"I don't have to justify myself to you," she snapped, glaring up at him with a razor-sharp look that should have sliced him to shreds. "You're *nothing* to me."

"Nothing?"

Call it arrogance, but he couldn't believe her. Even he had been surprised at the intensity of the erotic sizzle between them. Such instant awareness was rare. It fueled a sudden recklessness in him.

"Oh, no, my fine lady. I wouldn't call it nothing," he said, bending his head.

"What are you doing?" Her voice was a breathless gasp.

"Clarifying the difference between *nothing* and *something*."

Her reactions were too slow. By the time she tried to push him away he'd captured the back of her head in one hand. His fingers sank into the satiny invitation of her hair, his other arm wrapping around her waist.

"Relax," he murmured, already anticipating the heady pleasure of her lips against his. "This won't hurt a bit."

All about the author...
Annie West

ANNIE WEST discovered romance early—her childhood best friend's house was an unending store of Harlequin books—and she's been addicted ever since.

Fortunately she found her own real-life romantic hero while studying at university, and she married him. After gaining (despite the distraction) an honors classics degree, Annie took a job in the public service. For years she wrote and redrafted and revised—government plans, letters for cabinet ministers and reports for parliament. Checking the text of a novel is so much more fun!

Annie started to write romance when she took leave to spend time with her children. Between school activities she produced her first novel. At the same time she discovered Romance Writers of Australia. Since then she's been active in RWAus writers' groups and competitions. She attends annual conferences, and loves the support she gets from so many other writers. Her first Harlequin novel came out in 2005.

Annie lives with her hero (still the same one) and her children at Lake Macquarie, north of Sydney, and spends her time fantasizing about gorgeous men and their love lives. It's hard work, but she has no regrets!

Annie loves to hear from readers. You can contact her via her website, www.annie-west.com, or at annie@annie-west.com.

Annie West

RAFE'S REDEMPTION

TORONTO NEW YORK LONDON
AMSTERDAM PARIS SYDNEY HAMBURG
STOCKHOLM ATHENS TOKYO MILAN MADRID
PRAGUE WARSAW BUDAPEST AUCKLAND

Recycling programs
for this product may
not exist in your area.

ISBN-13: 978-0-373-23802-6

RAFE'S REDEMPTION
Previously published in the U.K. as *The Billionaire's Bought Mistress*

First North American Publication 2011

RAFE'S REDEMPTION

With heartfelt thanks to some fine writing friends: Alison, Daisy, Fiona, Heather, Karen and Serena. You've been terrific!

CHAPTER ONE

THE cold rose up from the ground, seeping through Antonia's boots and into her bloodstream as she stood, immobile. Icy air stung her cheeks and caught the back of her throat when she breathed.

Through her dark glasses she surveyed the others. The minister's cheeks were apple-red, and his breath as he spoke came out in white puffs. Most of the small gathering had reddened noses from the crisp wind that swirled flurries of white around their ankles. Antonia watched as they surreptitiously shifted their feet, trying to keep warm.

Stuart Dexter stood farthest away, two spots of colour painting his aristocratic cheeks. She should be furious he was here, but she didn't have the energy even for that.

It was easier to study the mourners than to absorb the minister's sonorous words. The flow of Swiss German was intended to soothe, yet Antonia found no comfort in his platitudes. Despite the coffin being lowered into the dark hole at her feet, she felt divorced from the proceedings.

Her dad wasn't here. Not in that cramped box. She blinked, almost expecting to hear some whispered aside from him, as if he leaned over her shoulder. Some thoroughly outrageous statement, inappropriate but inevitably witty, that would make her lips tilt into a reluctant smile despite the solemnity of the occasion.

She swallowed a sudden constriction in her throat as she reminded herself she wouldn't hear his voice again.

Her beloved, full-of-life, ready-for-anything, daredevil of a father was gone. *He'd left her alone.*

Guilt clutched her heart. She'd failed him miserably. This was her fault.

The chill of the Swiss churchyard was nothing to the deep freeze inside Antonia's body. The cold that spread out from her bones and her heart was every bit as frigid as the air temperature.

Six days since the accident. She was used to the numbness now—even found comfort in it. For she suspected if her heart were to thaw the pain would be unbearable.

She lifted her gaze to the clear alpine sky. Beyond the village Antonia saw the steep white slope of a mountain. Could even make out a zigzag of road, snow poles marking its edges. From here she couldn't see the spot where the car had skidded, slid, and then tumbled down the slope.

A tremor shuddered through her and swiftly she averted her eyes.

Movement caught her attention on the other side of the churchyard. She peered at the figure, now motionless in the blue-black shadow of the church.

He didn't approach, but she sensed his intense regard. The height, the breadth of shoulder, his stance, proclaimed him a man at the height of his vigour. He stood straight and tall. Even from this distance she sensed power, strength, and a solidity that told her he would never meld easily into a crowd.

He moved into the sunlight and Antonia frowned. She'd seen that face before, just last week. *The evening this nightmare had begun.*

She'd agreed to meet Stuart Dexter alone, to discuss his concerns about her father, opting for the safety of a popular bar instead of sharing a meal in his suite. Yet in the quiet foyer he'd groped her, sliding his hands over her as he helped her with her jacket, urging her back to his place for a private 'party'.

Bile rose to her mouth as she remembered the smell of his vodka-laden breath, hot against her face, his heavy hand grasping at her breast.

And over his shoulder the face of this man. A disturbing sky-blue gaze had locked on the pair of them as the stranger's severe features drew tight in supercilious distaste. His eyebrows had crammed together in a black smudge of disapproval.

For an instant she'd thought he was going to flatten Stuart as he grabbed at her and she fought to keep them both upright against his unsteady weight. Stuart had been pawing at her bra by the time she'd finally forced him away.

By that time the stranger had vanished.

What was he doing here today?

His brows were tilted in a V. With his night-dark hair, long black coat and the stark lines of his face accentuated by the slanting morning light, he looked like a disapproving angel, come to supervise her father's interment.

A bubble of something that might have been hysteria rose, threatening her composure. Her dad had joked that he'd never make it through the pearly gates. Despite the wonderful things he'd achieved, he said he'd made too many mistakes and enjoyed life far too much.

Something about the stranger's smouldering intensity, the forbidding set of his jaw and his utterly still posture was uncanny, catching her breath in her raw throat.

He was no angel. That firm, sculpted mouth spoke of experience, not innocence. And despite his dour expression Antonia had seen in an instant that he was the sort of man who'd draw women like a magnet.

The sound of the minister clearing his throat attracted Antonia's attention. He was winding up the service, watching her expectantly. She forced herself to look down into the chasm at her feet, to the coffin lying at the bottom.

For a moment roiling emotions stirred deep inside. Her eyes prickled hot with the threat of tears.

Then, mercifully, the permafrost of numbness closed round her again. Wherever her father was, it wasn't here.

Bending quickly, she scraped up a little gravel and let it fall. The sound of it spattering against wood was loud in the stillness. Final.

Abruptly she turned and shook the minister's hand, thanking him in flawless German for the service. Then, without waiting to talk to any of the others present, she strode off towards the street.

She felt their eyes on her as she left. Heard their murmurs. And on the bare flesh of her nape a prickling sensation teased her, made her falter in mid-stride.

Antonia didn't turn round. An atavistic sense told her what it was: reaction to the stranger's laser-sharp stare.

Some people liked to gawk. Well, let him. She was beyond caring about anyone else right now.

'Ms Malleson, excuse me.'

Antonia paused, unbuttoning her coat, and looked across to the concierge's desk in a corner of the lobby.

'Herr Weber.' Not the concierge but the manager. She nodded and summoned a vague smile for the man who had been so kind and helpful this past week. 'How are you?'

'Very good, thank you.' His voice had lost its appealing local burr and he spoke formally, with a precision totally unlike his usual warm manner. 'Could we talk, please? *Privately.*'

He looked uncomfortable. The determined set of his mouth was at odds with his normally ready smile.

Instantly Antonia's brain clicked to alert. It was fourteen years since her mother's death—that dreadful time when her father had gone off the rails. But Antonia remembered it vividly. Her father's restless energy, the reckless expenditure—as if he'd been trying to hide his grief in a whirl of new faces and fast living.

Some things stayed with you. Even after all this time Antonia knew instantly the look of a creditor about to demand payment in full. Polite, but worried. Unwilling to broach the unpleasant subject, but grimly determined.

How long had they been here? Frantically she calculated the rate for the suite her father had insisted on and the money left in her account. The result wasn't pretty, but she knew better than to let her concern show.

Damn! She should have been prepared. But in the last few days nothing had seemed to matter. She'd gone through the motions of everyday life in a weird vacuum, barely noticing what went on around her.

'Of course, Herr Weber.' She curved her lips into a more convincing smile as she walked towards the open office door he'd indicated. 'I wanted to speak with you too. I'll be leaving here soon and I'd like to see the account.'

'Ah.' That was definitely relief in his round brown eyes. 'As you wish, Ms Malleson. I understand that you will want to go home now that...'

Now that her father had been buried.

For an instant fierce emotion gripped her heart, squeezing so hard she almost cried out from the pain. Her face froze in rictus paralysis. It took a supreme effort to force the smile back in place.

'That's right,' she murmured at last, her voice husky. 'It's time I went home.'

No need to share the fact that she didn't have a home. That the closest thing she'd had to one in fourteen years had been an English boarding school.

Home had been wherever her dad was. And now...

Herr Weber lowered his voice to a whisper. 'I'm sorry to bother you at this time, Ms Malleson, but I've been fielding calls from a number of businesses. I took it upon myself to say you couldn't be contacted yet, but—'

'It's all right, Herr Weber, I understand.' Her heart plunged. Not just the hotel, then. How many accounts had her father run up?

Suddenly it all clicked into place.

Antonia had been away when her father had received his latest cardiologist's report. She was sure now it had been worse news than expected.

Of course her father had kept that to himself. She'd known something was wrong, her father hadn't been himself, but she'd let him reassure her.

Pain twisted low in her stomach.

She should have realised.

She reached out to touch the manager's arm reassuringly. The poor man looked so guilty. It wasn't *his* fault Gavin Malleson had started living extravagantly beyond his means again. Just like in his youth, when he'd been the darling of the jet set, and again when grief for his wife had set him on a downward spiral.

Antonia nodded to the worried man beside her. 'I'm afraid that with my father's accident I've been remiss in settling his accounts.'

'That's completely understandable, Ms Malleson.' The manager bowed his head in a courtly gesture and motioned for her to precede him into his office.

As he closed the door behind them Antonia spied a flicker of movement in the far corner of the foyer. The swing of a black coat, the sure stride of long legs.

The stranger from the funeral.

Her heart hit a faltering beat and then resumed its rhythm. Antonia wondered about the coincidence of seeing him here, in her hotel. Then the door shut and she forced herself to focus on more immediate problems.

* * *

Rafe watched the door close discreetly behind them.

So that confirmed it. His first instinct about her had been right. She was short of cash, so she played on her beauty, flashing those dark velvet eyes and cosying up to a man old enough to be her father in order to manoeuvre her way out of trouble. There'd been no mistaking the intimate warmth of her smile, or her hand on the manager's arm, the subtle invitation of her soft, throaty voice as she agreed to a *private* meeting.

Disappointment tasted bitter on Rafe's tongue. And that fuelled his anger. Surely he'd learned all he needed to about avaricious women in the years since he'd made the rich list? He'd been the target of too many gold-diggers, using every trick they could find to snare his interest.

Had he been foolish enough to hope Antonia Malleson was different? One look had made him want to believe that cool, classic beauty was more than skin deep.

Rafe had seen her and instantly wanted her, craved her with a hunger that had stopped him in his tracks. He'd been in the act of shouldering his way to where she stood alone when someone had joined her. A man he knew only too well. Stuart Dexter: twice her age and with a reputation that would keep decent women away. His girlfriends all had one thing in common—a mercenary streak that overcame the revulsion they must feel in his bed.

Since then Rafe had gathered details about this

woman who still, to his chagrin, drew his gaze and heated his blood. She lived a life of pleasure, trailing from one expensive resort to another. Obviously she had no qualms about trading on her looks to secure a wealthy lover. Only last week Rafe had seen her and Dexter at a nightclub known for its ready supply of designer drugs. She'd let Dexter half undress her as they'd swayed drunkenly together.

No, she was as shallow as the rest of that crowd. Self-absorbed and greedy.

Just like Stuart Dexter.

Rafe's long-lost, not-at-all-lamented father.

When Rafe had seen her at the graveside this morning, pale and still and composed, she'd been like an ice princess, aloof and remote. As if the loss of her father meant nothing to her. He'd wondered if it could be true what the gossips said: that she was cold at heart. No lasting relationship with a man. No host of female friends.

Then he'd looked more closely. Had that been a hint of vulnerability behind her reserve? She'd looked brittle, as if she held back her grief only by desperate self-control.

And even then Rafe had wanted her.

The hunger he'd felt when he'd first seen her had morphed now into a blood-deep need. Its impact still rocked him, like a pounding blow to the chest.

Lust shouldn't be on his agenda. He had other, more important things on his mind.

Rafe hadn't understood the compulsion to follow

her from the churchyard. He'd told himself he wanted to stretch his legs as he walked up the road to the hotel, leaving his rental car behind. It had nothing to do with unwilling concern for a girl who looked to be deep in shock.

But what he'd just seen had dispelled that illusion.

Rafe eyed the closed door to the manager's office and felt a twist of revulsion in the pit of his belly. Obviously the fact that she'd just buried her father meant little to her. Certainly not enough to prevent her playing manipulative games for her own ends.

He turned on his heel and strode out through the entrance.

The cold, distant look he'd seen on her face in the graveyard summed her up. She wasn't suffering from shock or grief at all.

Antonia Malleson had shown her true colours. And in doing so she'd provided him with a perfect weapon. He had no compunction about using it to his own advantage. The bonus would be the personal satisfaction he'd derive from turning the tables on the beautiful little gold digger.

'I'm sorry, Ms Malleson. Your father's annuity ended with his death. There will be no more payments.'

Antonia sat rigidly upright beside the writing desk. This wasn't news, she told herself. It merely confirmed what she'd suspected. All the same, it was a blow. Her fingers tightened around the receiver.

'I understand,' she said wearily. 'Thank you.'

'Of course,' her father's lawyer explained, in his carefully modulated tone, 'once probate is finalised, as Gavin Malleson's sole heir his assets will pass to you.'

His assets. That almost made her laugh.

Her dad had never been one to scrimp and save. He'd lived lavishly. And if ever there had been money to spare it had gone to the Claudia Benzoni Foundation, the charity he'd established twelve years ago to support victims of the rare cancer that had killed his beloved wife.

Antonia had managed her father's inadequate budget, supplementing it from her summer earnings as a tour guide and interpreter. She knew how little was in his account.

Not for the first time she wished she'd been able to work full-time and put aside some more substantial savings. But her father had needed her, his health deteriorating so badly she'd been scared to leave him alone too long.

'I'm afraid it will take some time to finalise.'

It didn't matter. Her father's legacy consisted solely of debts. She'd contacted the solicitor in the vain hope of finding a way to pay them.

'Thank you very much,' she said. 'I appreciate you clarifying the details for me.'

'I'm happy to help, Ms Malleson. If there's anything else I can do to assist, please contact me.'

Antonia put the phone down slowly. Where did

she go from here? The funeral had wiped out her savings. Even when she sold her mother's jewellery she'd have trouble covering the bills. There was more than just the hotel to be paid.

A band of tension clamping tight around her chest reminded her to breathe. The dull throb of pain in her temples sharpened. She stumbled to her feet, knowing she needed to *do* something, if only pace the room.

She was alone in this.

Antonia thought of her dad's car, crumpled and charred at the base of a cliff. A shudder rippled through her.

It was her fault. All her fault.

A sob rose in her throat. She should have *been* there with him. She'd promised to drive him that morning. Had arranged to meet him early. But she'd let him down.

He was dead because of her. Guilt racked her. She clenched her hands, remembering.

It had started with Stuart Dexter. For the last fortnight wherever she'd turned there he'd been, watching her with a hunger that made her skin crawl. She'd only gone out with him that night because she'd fallen for his line about discussing concerns for her father.

She'd fended him off at the nightclub, thought she could handle him. That was before he'd offered to drive her back to the hotel and she'd been foolish enough to agree.

In the dark confines of the car he'd lunged at her, using his weight and the cramped space to pin her beneath him. He'd tried to force her into intimacy. She'd only just escaped, her shirt torn and her heart pounding in distress and fear. She'd spent the night pacing, wondering whether to call the police, wondering how to tell her dad the man he trusted had attacked her. Eventually sleep had claimed her around dawn, and she'd slept through the alarm. *Slept till the police came to the door with news of her father.*

If only she'd been there that morning there would have been no accident. He wouldn't have died alone.

The walls closed in as horror stifled her breath and blurred her vision.

In a surge of energy she pocketed her key card, grabbed her coat and plunged out of the door. Not bothering with the lift, she hurried down the stairs and into the foyer, desperate to get outside, into the fresh air.

'Careful!' A deep voice growled in her ears. Strong hands on her arms pulled her up short as she catapulted into the hard, warm wall of a masculine chest.

Antonia inhaled a new scent, subtle and spicy, and felt the warmth of it unfurl in her lungs. Her hands splayed against finest cashmere in a deep blue. The heat of his chest penetrated her palms, shocking her into tingling awareness. She hadn't felt anything so warm in a week.

Automatically she went to step back, but his grip held firm, not releasing her. Frowning, she looked up.

At a few inches under six feet, she was usually at eye level with most men. Yet her gaze lifted higher and higher. This man must be over half a foot taller than she was.

But it wasn't his height, or even his impressive shoulders that made Antonia stare. It was the way his azure-blue gaze held hers. Heat shimmered between them, a tangible yet invisible link.

Her eyes widened at the instant connection.

It was him. The man she'd seen at the club that night and again yesterday. He'd watched the funeral. She'd caught a glimpse of him several times before that too, but always at a distance.

A safe distance.

For there was something in his eyes that spoke of danger. A focus, an awareness that panicked her, made her want to thrash out of his hold and flee back to the sanctuary of her room.

Her heartbeat thudded loud in her ears and her breath caught on an indrawn hiss.

It wasn't simply fear of the unknown she felt. Nor even reaction to the absolute focus of his stare. It was the instant realisation that she was *drawn* to him. To this stranger with the bold face now set hard in stern lines.

Emotion swirled and rippled through her. Meeting

those eyes was like waking from a foggy dream to face stunning reality.

'You can let me go now.' Her voice was a husky whisper and she swallowed, trying to moisten her dry mouth.

His eyes followed the convulsive movement, and Antonia almost choked as a rush of heat scalded her throat. The air between them sizzled. How could his long silent look be so…aware? So sexually potent?

His gaze trawled up to her mouth and Antonia's breathing grew shallow.

It was her imagination. It had to be. She'd been stared at by lots of men, but she'd never felt anything like this. Obviously her emotions were haywire after the stress of this last week.

Antonia pulled back, as if she could break his hold. Anxiety skittered up her spine as his large hands remained where they were, warmly encircling her upper arms.

Then his eyes met hers, and she realised he'd read her fear. One dark eyebrow arched up on his tanned face. His hands dropped away.

And still he didn't speak. Belatedly Antonia realised that her hands remained spread across his chest. Her fingers had even curled into the fine wool, as if to anchor her close to the solid wall of muscle beneath. The steady beat of his heart vibrated against her right palm.

Hastily Antonia lifted her hands and stepped back. Instantly the bustle of new arrivals intruded into her consciousness. The sound of a child giggling, and of a mixture of voices conversing in French, German and Spanish.

There was a blur of movement in the periphery of her vision, yet her gaze remained snagged on his.

'Ms Malleson.' His voice was a deep rumble that prickled the hairs on her nape. 'How fortuitous.'

The skittish impulse to run still pumped through her veins. Antonia ignored it. Despite the disturbing fact that he knew her name, there could be nothing to fear from him here in a busy hotel foyer.

'I'm afraid you have the advantage of me, Mr...'

'Benton. Rafe Benton.'

There was something about his voice that tweaked her curiosity. Not just its richness, but the hint of an accent. Not British, though close. Not American either.

Instinct told her it would be safer not to indulge her curiosity. Far better to put some distance between them.

'Well, Mr Benton, I'm on my way out so—'

'You're going out in that?'

She followed his gaze and saw a blur of white outside the windows. They were in the middle of a snowstorm and she hadn't noticed. No fresh air for her, then. She'd have to pace her room while she worked through her problems.

'Maybe not.' She turned, ready to head up the stairs.

'Wait.' He spoke quietly, yet instinctively Antonia

responded to his tone of command. She paused with her foot on the first step.

'I want to talk with you.'

Slowly she turned, unwilling to face that pinioning blue gaze. Then she summoned her courage and met his eyes. His scrutiny seared her but she refused to be cowed.

'I can't imagine why.'

'Can't you?'

'No.'

Maybe with those killer looks and that untamed air he was used to women fawning over him.

Antonia wasn't in the mood. Despite what her uneven pulse might indicate, she wasn't impressed. She'd had enough of men who saw her as a commodity to be possessed.

'Now, if you'll excuse me, Mr Benton, I'll—'

'And what if I don't? Excuse you, that is.'

What? Antonia felt her jaw loosen in surprise. Who did he think he was?

She'd placed that trace of an accent now. Faint but distinctive. This brash stranger was Australian. Yet surely they learned basic courtesy Down Under?

'What's your problem?' she asked bluntly, more bluntly than usual. Something about this man sliced right through the social niceties. Had he been following her?

She glanced across to Herr Weber, busy supervising his staff in the foyer. The sight was reassuring. She only had to call out if she needed help.

Rafe Benton crossed his arms over his chest. The action emphasised the sheer physicality of his big frame. Antonia stood firm against the desire to back away a pace.

'No problem. Not for *me*.'

Had she imagined his emphasis on the last word?

'I have business to discuss with you.'

Ah, that was it. One of her father's creditors. It was almost a relief to identify him as something so mundane—though it meant another bill to pay. For a moment there she'd been really unnerved by his unblinking scrutiny.

'*Private* business,' he reiterated.

Antonia drew a slow breath and stiffened her spine. 'Of course,' she said finally. 'Let's go to the lounge and we can discuss your business.'

He didn't budge, merely shook his head. 'What I have to say is private. The lounge and bar are full of people avoiding the bad weather.'

And there was no privacy to be had here in the foyer.

'Then let's schedule our meeting for later—'

'This can't wait. Your suite is private. We'll go there.' He gestured to the stairs behind her. 'Unless you'd rather take the lift?'

He had a nerve, inviting himself to her room. As if she was in the habit of letting strangers into her private space. Especially strangers like him, who exuded testosterone the way a blaze gave off heat.

'That's not possible.' Her voice was jerky with indignation.

'Oh, I think you'll find it more than possible, Ms Malleson.' His voice lowered to a deep purr that brushed across her skin like velvet. Yet there was an undertone of honed steel. 'In fact, I'd call it advisable.'

She was shaking her head when he reached into his pocket and took out a paper. He held it in front of her.

It was a receipt from a hotel. *This* hotel.

Antonia's jaw sagged as she read it, then reread it. What she saw there turned her pulse into a racing tattoo. Finally, reluctantly, she lifted her eyes to his.

Rafe Benton had paid, in cash, for the suite she and her father had occupied these last weeks. Not only had he covered the outstanding amount, but he'd paid for the rooms up till the end of the week.

'I've bought your debt, Ms Malleson. I think you agree I have a right to see the rooms I've paid for. Don't you?'

CHAPTER TWO

His large hand was firm as he urged her towards the stairs. Antonia dug her heels in. Across the foyer she saw Herr Weber, and lifted her hand to signal for assistance.

The manager caught her glance, but instead of coming to her aid he looked embarrassed, a dull flush colouring his cheeks. Quickly he turned to speak to the concierge.

Slowly Antonia's hand dropped to her side.

'You won't get any help from your admirer Weber.' Rafe Benton's tone was dismissive. 'Once he understood I was paying, he realised you were off-limits.'

Off-limits? Antonia's head whirled as she tried to absorb what he was saying.

'You mean he thinks we're…? That you've paid this because…?'

'It doesn't matter what he thinks,' Rafe Benton said. 'Just that he understands this is between you and me.'

'*What?*' She spun round to face him. 'What is

between us? I don't *know* you. Why should you pay for my suite?'

'Why don't we go upstairs and discuss this away from curious ears?'

Antonia saw the tilt of his head towards the other side of the room, where a couple had emerged from the restaurant and watched them with barely concealed interest.

Rafe looked down into her startled face. There was colour in her cheeks now, and it suited her. No longer the ice queen.

Slowly she turned, and he saw fire spark golden in her brown eyes. Her full, cupid's bow lips primmed into a narrow line of displeasure. Her stare might have shrivelled a lesser man to cinders. It was the sort of look the moneyed elite reserved for upstart underlings.

He repressed a smile as anticipation stirred deep in his belly. And lower.

She'd learn.

It would give him great pleasure to educate Antonia Malleson about the wielding of real power. Call it an added perk, but right now the idea of teaching her a lesson in humility was almost as gratifying as the prospect of his larger, far more important plans.

He was human enough, man enough, to enjoy the prospect of her compliance. Of bending her to his will and his pleasure.

Oh, yes. Already he was looking forward to *that*.

'Let me assure you I have no intention of ravishing you as soon as we get over the threshold.' He watched her eyes widen and her mouth round in astonishment.

'I still don't—'

'I'm not a patient man, Ms Malleson, and I don't have much time. I'll give you a choice. We can sort this out in the privacy of your apartments. Or we can do it right here, within earshot of whoever happens to be passing.'

Of course she capitulated. Yet it was fascinating watching pride war with common sense in those lustrous eyes. She took her time about agreeing. A full thirty seconds. He counted them.

Selfish, shallow, mercenary—just like Dexter. She was the perfect tool for revenge against his father.

But, more than that, Antonia Malleson was fast becoming a very private challenge.

Antonia swiped her room card and pushed open the door, conscious of his looming presence behind her. She told herself he deliberately used his size to intimidate her. A hint of threat hung between them, but she ignored it, assuring herself his aggressive air was intentional—part of his plan to get back the money her father owed.

But if he was a creditor, why pay her account?

Whatever his purpose, he wouldn't harm her. There'd been witnesses to their meeting downstairs.

Then she remembered how Herr Weber had avoided eye contact, and a thread of anxiety spun through her.

'Are we going in, or do you intend to discuss our business here in the corridor?'

Antonia's slumping shoulders straightened at the sarcasm in his voice. She entered the room, flicking on the lights, and stood aside, gesturing for him to precede her.

Silently he strode past her, straight to the centre of the sitting room. There he stood, taking in the luxurious suite. The traditional woodwork that teamed surprisingly well with the latest Italian leather lounge furniture. The air of refined yet sumptuous comfort that attracted a steady clientele to this prestigious boutique hotel.

'Very pleasant,' he murmured, glancing at the state-of-the-art entertainment unit that took up one vast wall.

Antonia didn't miss the edge of cynicism in his words, but she had more important things to worry about.

'Who *are* you?' She shut the door and walked across the room to stand watching him.

'I told you. Rafe Benton.' He strolled to the other side of the room and, without asking, straight into a bedroom. She hurried to the doorway, watching him give the luxurious bathroom a cursory glance, then turn his attention to the vast bed with its ivory satin spread.

Her hands curled into fists at his presumption and at the knowledge she couldn't eject him from the premises. He was infinitely stronger than she, and the hard edge to his jaw, the expression on his brooding face, told her she'd be a fool to try pushing him out of the door.

She had no hope of getting him to leave until he'd said whatever he had to say.

'*What* are you, then?' A professional debt collector? He had the daunting power to persuade anyone to cough up money they owed. Yet his clothes were of the finest quality—made to measure, if she was any judge. Besides, he looked like a man used to giving orders, not roughing up recalcitrant debtors.

He slanted an inscrutable look from under dark brows and she stiffened.

'I'm the man who's paid for your accommodation here. That gives me the right to inspect the… premises.'

But it wasn't the premises he was surveying. His gaze dropped from hers, lingered on her lips, then slowly, infinitesimally slowly, travelled down her dark sweater, over the swell of her hips and further, all the way to her boots. That look made her wish she hadn't dropped her overcoat onto a chair. It made her feel that there was nothing protecting her from his inspection.

Beneath the plain cotton of her bra, the comfortable stretch fabric of her top and the light knit of her sweater, her nipples puckered and tightened.

Her breasts felt heavy, as if weighted by his look. A strange tingling sensation spread across her chest, and lower.

Panic flared as she tried to rationalise her body's reaction. She couldn't be aroused by his blatant stare, could she?

Then, suddenly, she was looking straight into vivid blue eyes that had lost their chilly reserve. A jolt of energy sheared through her, tightening every muscle.

'This looks very comfortable,' he murmured, his gesture encompassing the room, but most especially the wide bed right beside him. 'Will we have our chat here?'

'No!' She almost choked on the word. 'We'll use the sitting room.' Antonia spun round and stalked out, ignoring what could have been a low chuckle behind her.

This had gone far enough. No matter who he was, the man had no right to bait her. She went straight to the phone and lifted the receiver.

'I wouldn't do that, if I were you.' Suddenly Rafe Benton was beside her. He didn't reach out, but she stilled.

'Tell me what you want or I'll have the police up here.'

He raised his brows as if in surprise, then nodded. 'All right. Take a seat.'

Without waiting for her, he subsided onto one of the long sofas. The black leather was a perfect foil for the deep blue of his sweater, and for those eyes that surveyed her so steadily.

Antonia put the receiver down and sat on a nearby chair. She perched upright on the edge of the seat.

'I have a proposition for you.'

She frowned. That didn't sound like a creditor.

'Go on.'

'I've paid your account here as a sign of my goodwill.'

Looking at his long body, sprawled so comfortably across the sofa, Antonia read assurance, power and easy confidence. No sign of anything as soft or generous as goodwill. Though in the depth of that suddenly hooded gaze there was something else, and it made her blood pump faster. Some spark of…excitement? No. Anticipation.

'Go on,' she urged, watching him with a wary, unblinking stare.

'I'll be in Europe for the next six months. Mainly in London.' With one outstretched hand he drew lazy circles on the fine-grained leather. His fingers were long, supple and slow moving. For a crazy moment Antonia felt a circle of heat on the bare flesh of her neck, as if he'd touched her.

Her breath shortened, but she sat rigidly still, waiting.

'I'll be working most of the time, but I'll want some company too. Feminine company.'

Antonia's forehead knitted in confusion. He was *lonely*?

She rejected the idea instantly. For all his insolent demeanour, his deliberate rejection of the social niceties, Rafe Benton wasn't the sort to pine for companionship. She'd bet all the money she didn't have that he was usually the centre of attention. He had the indisputable take-charge air of a leader—of someone who didn't give two pins for what others thought or did. His bold looks would bring women flocking to him. All he'd have to do was click his fingers and he'd be surrounded by feminine company.

'I'm afraid you've lost me.'

His lips curved up in a tantalising glimmer of a smile. Just a hint of one. Antonia sucked in her breath as its force hit her and shock waves rippled through her unprepared body.

It wasn't a warm smile, or a friendly one. There was an edge of mockery to it, an almost wolfish sharpness that made him look far too predatory. Yet still she was mesmerised, watching breathlessly as his eyes glittered brighter. Grooves appeared, bracketing his firm mouth, enhancing the strong symmetry of his features.

What would be the effect if he smiled in genuine affection or amusement?

'Ah, then I'll cut straight to the chase.' His fingers stilled against the back of the sofa and she sensed his focus sharpen, though he didn't appear to move a muscle.

'I want you to become my mistress.'

Antonia blinked, focusing on his lips. Had she heard him right? Surely not. It was impossible.

'I'm sorry, I—'

'No need to be sorry, sweetheart. All you have to do is say yes.'

'I…' Her breath escaped on a sigh of disbelief. She curled her hands into fists, pressing her fingernails against her palms, as if that prickling pain could wake her from this bizarre nightmare. 'I don't even *know* you!'

'Ah, I was forgetting. Where I come from I don't have much need of introduction.' He stretched his legs out. 'Rafe Benton. Thirty. Australian. CEO of Pacifica Holdings. I live in Brisbane, but I also have apartments in New York and Tokyo. Bank balance—' his eyes narrowed '—healthy enough to keep you in luxury.'

He paused, as if waiting for her to respond. But for the life of her Antonia was speechless. *Her*, a rich man's mistress? The idea was outrageous.

'I like my women good-looking, intelligent and amenable. I don't have patience for tantrums or tears, and I expect absolute exclusivity. I don't share.' His eyes flashed a warning. 'I want a companion who can hold her own in any social situation: formal dinners, business functions and balls. Someone with the requisite social graces.'

She moistened her lips to speak, to stop him, but he continued regardless.

'My tastes are relatively simple. I expect passion in

a lover.' Again that feral half-smile that sent a tingle of warning through her. 'I'm not into anything kinky. Though I'm more than willing to experiment.' His voice deepened. 'In appropriate circumstances.'

The tingle morphed into a shudder as his gaze travelled over her and heat licked her skin. More, a tiny twist of feminine response awakened deep inside her dormant body.

Antonia was appalled.

'In return you'd have six months of living totally at my expense—and I can be very generous if I'm satisfied.'

The glitter in his eyes told her he was talking about sex. What else?

The silence lengthened as Antonia absorbed the shock reverberating through her.

Who the hell did he think she was?

'I'm not some cheap tart,' she blurted out when she eventually found her voice.

'Of course not, sweetheart. I didn't for a moment think there was anything cheap about you.'

'Don't call me *sweetheart*!' Raw fury lent volume to her voice. Her suddenly unlocked emotions roiled to the surface and she felt overwhelmingly, gloriously furious. The ice-cold numbness of the last week had shattered, smashed by a flood of hatred for this arrogant, self-opinionated jerk. She shot to her feet, hands on her hips as she stared down at his rangy form sprawled so indolently before her.

'What do you think gives you the right to insult me like that?'

'Hardly an insult. Simply a business proposition.'

Unbelievable! She'd never met a man with such gall.

Antonia's heart thudded painfully hard, its rhythm jerky and out of kilter.

'Then you can take your business elsewhere. I don't know how things are done in Australia, but you're way out of line here. I'm not for sale.'

Slowly he tucked his long legs under him and rose to his full height. At any other time the force of the warning look in his eyes might have made her step away, but not now. She was beyond anything as mundane as caution.

'Ah. My mistake.' He shrugged those broad shoulders. 'I overheard some of your conversation with the manager and I know you're short of cash. You have a wait till the next quarter's allowance comes through.' He paused. 'What happened? Did you spend it all on designer clothes and parties? Or do you have more expensive habits? You don't look like a user, but it can be hard to tell.'

His mock sympathy made her grit her teeth. How dared he talk to her like that? She wasn't going to share intimate information with him. Like the fact that she didn't have an allowance and she was virtually destitute.

'My finances aren't your concern. Nor are my

habits. But let me put your mind at rest. I don't use drugs.'

'Good. I thought you too intelligent for that. As for the cash…' He raised his hand, as if placating her. 'Of course you won't have a problem paying me what you owe for this luxurious accommodation. Or your other debts.'

'Other debts?' Her indignation bled away.

'Your friend Weber helpfully mentioned your creditors.' His teeth flashed in a ruthless smile. 'I've done you a favour and bought the debts. Now you only have one creditor to deal with: me.'

Antonia's heart plunged. No wonder she'd had trouble tracking down all the money her father owed.

'How much are they worth?'

'You don't know?' One dark eyebrow rose. 'Enough. I'll send you a full account.'

Her throat closed as she saw the implacable light in his eyes. She knew the amount was large—larger than she could manage. And this man was no benefactor.

'Does your silence mean you *can't* pay me?'

'I…' She swallowed her pride, wishing she could tell him to go to hell. 'Are you saying you'll demand payment?'

She held her breath as he surveyed her. A swift, calculating look that made her want to cringe. But she had to face him down. Instinctively she understood that she couldn't let him see how threatened she felt.

'The debt is genuine. Of course it has to be paid.' He paused, and she heard the blood rush in her ears. 'Though if you were my mistress I'd feel obliged to write it off.'

A spasm of shock tightened Antonia's body.

'Why me?' she said abruptly, her head spinning. Surely a man with his looks and wealth didn't need to buy a lover?

He paced closer. Suddenly the room seemed short of oxygen, as if his proximity sucked the air from her lungs.

'I saw you and I wanted you.'

To her horrified disbelief the simple statement evoked a tremor of unwanted excitement, piercing right through the very core of her.

He reached out and stroked his index finger from her temple down her cheek, lingering at the corner of her mouth, where a flicker of response trembled across her nerve-endings. Then he slid his hand down, cupping her chin in his warm palm, raising her face so that she met the full force of his glittering stare.

Her pulse jerked erratically and her breath came in short, distressed puffs that she couldn't control. His spicy scent was heady and enticing, reminding her of the way his hard body had felt when they'd collided. Strong. Masculine. Tempting.

What was happening to her? According to the men

she'd dated, she was far too reserved. Too unaffected by the lure of pheromones and a healthy male.

The way her body revved into full awareness, just from being close to Rafe Benton, was unprecedented.

'It's no crime for a man to go for what he wants,' he murmured, his head tilting infinitesimally closer. 'Or would you prefer I dressed this up with pretty words that don't mean anything? Pretend I'm looking for something longer term? Lie to you about my intentions?'

'No!' To her horror, Antonia was mesmerised by the way his mouth moved as he spoke, his lips almost hypnotic while he whispered his outrageous questions. His voice had lowered to a burr that raised the hairs on her arms, as if her body expected... something.

'Good. I prefer to say what I think. It saves a lot of time.' His lips quirked in a way that brought those sexy grooves to the corners of his mouth.

Antonia expelled the breath she'd unconsciously held. Desperately she reminded herself that he was everything she despised: pushy, domineering, acting like God's gift to women. As if she was his for the asking.

'So, Ms Malleson. You don't like what I have to say. But you don't want to pay your debt.' Slowly he shook his head. 'I have to say I'm disappointed.'

Antonia's tongue cleaved to the roof of her mouth as embarrassment heated her cheeks and throat.

'First I need to see the paperwork. Perhaps then we could discuss a schedule of payments?'

His eyes narrowed.

'Did I mention that if you stay as my mistress for six months, not only will I cancel your debt, I'll provide a substantial cash settlement when we part?'

He tilted his head, and for a horrified moment she thought he was going to kiss her. Instead his lips grazed her ear, his breath a hot, disturbingly erotic caress as he whispered a sum so large it made her freeze in disbelief.

'You have to be kidding!'

'I don't joke about my money. Or my women,' he murmured. Then his teeth closed round her earlobe and he tugged gently, provocatively. Instantly darts of fire arrowed to her nipples, her groin, and she caught her breath on an audible gasp. Such a tiny scrape of teeth on flesh and yet she felt branded.

'Don't!' She shoved at his shoulders. It was like trying to push away a boulder.

'Sorry.' He didn't sound at all apologetic. 'Did I hurt you?' His tongue flicked out to soothe the place where his teeth had grazed her.

Something shifted in the pit of Antonia's stomach and her knees began to melt. Her hands curved in against his shoulders, seeking support as she sagged.

'Is that a no?'

She jerked her head away, appalled at this uncharacteristic weakness flooding her. She'd never felt anything like it.

What had he done to her?

His proposition was an insult, his attitude obnoxious. He made her fume at his arrogance. Yet her body responded blatantly, hungrily to his touch.

'I want you to leave. *Now!*'

She felt him straighten, his hand drop from her chin. Yet the warmth of his touch lingered, marking her skin. Belatedly she let go of his shoulders, furious that she had so few defences against his raw physical allure.

'Tell me one thing.' His voice seemed to come from a long way above her.

'What?' Antonia refused to look at him, choosing instead to focus on the blur of white outside the window.

'Why are you refusing me?'

She looked up at that, stunned that he even had to ask. Anger surged again, thankfully replacing that absurd weakness in her blood.

'You think I'm in the habit of sleeping with men for money?'

He shrugged. 'You've been keeping Stuart Dexter company, but you don't have the dewy-eyed look of a woman in love. He must be thirty years your senior. Don't tell me his fatal charm attracted you. It has to be his money. After all—' he flicked a glance around the luxurious room '—you definitely have champagne tastes.'

Antonia took a step back from him, hands grasped together so tightly they shook.

'Well? Are you going to deny it?'

He thought she was *encouraging* Dexter?

The idea was risible. She'd only put up with Stuart's presence because of her father. Dexter was involved in the financial management of the charity that had meant so much to her dad.

Antonia blinked to clear her vision. For two weeks she'd suffered Stuart's leers and his smarmy suggestions for the sake of her father. Nothing else. After what he'd done, just the thought of the man curdled her stomach.

Rafe stared down into her averted face and knew he'd hit a nerve. It didn't take the pulse jerking at the base of her neck or the flat line of her compressed lips to give her away.

He'd seen her rich brown eyes shimmer, overbright, before she turned her head away.

Vulnerability? From someone mercenary enough to target a wealthy man so she could have an easy life?

He wondered.

No. She was a superlative actress. Playing on a man's sympathy was part of her stock in trade, especially with her damnably beautiful face. She must have used a trick or two to hook Dexter—the man was obsessed with her. It was obvious from the way he watched her every move, with a raw appetite that turned Rafe's stomach.

Yet obviously his father wasn't generous enough with his money, since she was short of cash. No doubt Dexter's looming financial woes were restricting his expenditure. Rafe intended to take advantage of that fact.

Why didn't she accept the proposition he'd just offered her? That intrigued him. Was she holding out for a better offer?

He'd felt her reaction as he caressed her earlobe. She hadn't been able to conceal the tremor of desire that juddered through her. Her instant, undeniable reaction had been an incredible turn-on. His body had hardened immediately as he'd realised what a sensuous, responsive woman Antonia Malleson was.

'You're not denying it,' he taunted.

'I don't have to justify myself to you,' she snapped, glaring up at him with a razor-sharp look that should have sliced him to shreds. 'You're *nothing* to me.'

'Nothing?'

Call it arrogance, but he couldn't believe her. Even he had been surprised at the intensity of the erotic sizzle between them. Such instant awareness was rare. It fuelled a sudden recklessness in him.

'Oh, no, my fine lady. I wouldn't call it nothing,' he said, bending his head.

'What are you doing?' Her voice was a breathless gasp.

'Clarifying the difference between *nothing* and *something*.'

Her reactions were too slow. By the time she tried to push him away he'd captured the back of her head in one hand. His fingers sank into the satiny invitation of her hair, his other arm wrapping round her waist.

'Relax,' he murmured, already anticipating the heady pleasure of her lips against his. 'This won't hurt a bit.'

CHAPTER THREE

HIS mouth on hers muffled Antonia's scathing retort.

She struggled against him, but his hold was implacable, unbreakable. The more she tried to get free, the more restrictive was his embrace. A granite cliff would have been more pliable than this mountain of a man.

Who did he think he was, with his outrageous proposition and now his use of superior strength to force a kiss?

Tension spiralled through her as he crowded near, his thighs surrounding hers, his mouth against her closed lips, his hand anchoring her head, one long, strong arm wrapped around her waist.

He was so close, held her so immobile, that she couldn't even get leverage to bring her knee up against him. He contained her struggling form with mortifying ease.

Finally she realised resistance was futile. She held herself stiff as a board, keeping her eyes wide open, refusing to capitulate.

Strangely, it was annoyance she felt. Outrage, not fear. Not like when Dexter had groped her and panic had swelled, making her frantic to escape.

Rafe Benton was more subtle, for all his apparent directness. This man was a wily tactician, a long-term strategist. Not a smash and grab thug like Dexter.

It took her several moments to realise he wasn't using force. His hold was firm, but not tight. His arm at her back held her close, but not brutally so. He seemed content to tease her lips with a gentle, coaxing caress, rather than bruise her into surrender.

All she had to do was stand here, still and unyielding, and he'd stop soon.

She hoped he'd stop soon.

Something about the encompassing warmth of his body threatened to make her relax into his embrace. His lips were surprisingly soft, surprisingly tender.

He took her bottom lip between his teeth, tugging gently, and sensation shot through her, straight down to her breasts, then lower, arrowing to her feminine core.

Antonia started, horrified at the fizz of awareness building in her blood. Like a slow, betraying sizzle.

She pushed her hands against his chest, trying to propel him back, away from her. He was immovable. She splayed her fingers wide and tried again. Nothing. Just the steady beat of his life pulse beneath her fingers.

'Mmm,' he murmured against her mouth. 'Touch me.'

Touch him? She'd give him more than a touch when she'd finished with him!

'I—'

Her pithy retort turned into a mumbled moan as she realised her mistake. His tongue slipped into her mouth as she opened her lips and suddenly the world rocked on its foundations. His arm at her back, his legs surrounding hers, were the only supports keeping her upright.

Antonia's head swam as he delved in, caressing her tongue, her mouth, with a seductively insistent expertise that made warning bells jangle in her ears.

It felt…it felt… Thought atrophied as pleasure mounted. Antonia struggled to escape the fog of sheer physical enjoyment that he'd conjured. She fought not to respond to the slow, evocative caress of his mouth, his teasing tongue, his seductive lips.

She battled the liquid heat of desire that spread through her loosening body and blazed a trail of fire to the secret place between her legs. She squeezed her thighs together, trying to counteract the ache that made her want to melt against him and demand more.

She tried to focus on something else. On the dark gleaming hair, combed ruthlessly back from his face. On the intriguing scent of his skin, spicy, but now overlaid with a hint of musk that made her nostrils flare.

No!

She could withstand this onslaught. Her pride depended on it. Despite the incredible sensations of warmth and pleasure his kiss evoked, the promise of sheer ecstasy.

His hand moved in her hair, tugging at her neat chignon, threading through the long tresses as they tumbled round her shoulders. His touch was leisurely, as if he enjoyed the caress as much as she. He massaged her scalp and her eyelids lowered, her fingers holding onto the soft wool of his pullover.

He bent her back against his arm. Now he had unfettered access, kissing her with a thoroughness that obliterated everything except the recognition of pleasure.

Antonia moaned as his tongue danced against hers and her nipples hardened, eager for the brush of his hard chest. Her eyes flickered shut as she gave herself up to the inevitable, to burgeoning delight. To the sheer comfort of being held safe in strong arms, rocked close against his solid body. To the building excitement of a kiss that was now mutual.

Somehow her hands had slid up and over his shoulders, to lock in the silky softness of his hair, to mould his skull with fingers that trembled. She angled her mouth against his, pressing close as need notched higher and her pulse accelerated into overdrive.

Then, without warning, he stepped away. The lush, sensuous pleasure ended abruptly and cool air rushed in between them. His hands moved to her shoulders, as if he knew she needed support to stand upright.

She resented the fact that she did. Her knees quivered and her legs felt like jelly. A wave of horror flooded her as she realised she'd not only let him kiss her, but had given herself up to his embrace. For a moment she'd even found *comfort* in his closeness!

She looked up at him through slitted eyes and realised he was as cool and distant as before.

All except for the flared nostrils and the pronounced movement of his chest as he dragged in deep breaths.

It was small consolation to see he'd been affected too. She felt dizzy, shocked by his audacity and by the depth of her own response. How could that have happened?

'No, you're wrong,' he murmured, with a smugness that made Antonia want to jam her fist into the hard wall of his abdomen. 'I wouldn't say there was *nothing* between us.' He tilted his head to one side, as if musing. 'In fact I'd say we definitely had something going there.'

Antonia's wrath almost boiled over then. But she knew that any further loss of control on her part would be a victory for this brute.

'You've got to be joking.' It cost her a lot to keep her voice cool and casual, not overplay her hand. 'I was just curious to see if your over-sized ego made a difference to the way you kiss.'

Brilliant fire blazed in his blue gaze and she hurried on, turning to put some much-needed distance between them.

'As for having something going...' She paused, surreptitiously clearing her throat. 'That would be you, Mr Benton.' She stepped away, hoping he couldn't see how badly her legs shook. 'It's time for you to leave.'

Carefully she walked to the entrance and pulled the door open, her hand clammy on the doorknob.

For endless seconds there was no sound but the rapid thud of her pulse echoing in her ears. He didn't move, but stood in the centre of the room, watching her. She refused to meet his gaze. If she did she knew her poise would crumble as a hot tide of mortification flooded her cheeks.

Please. Let him go. Antonia didn't have the strength to deal with him. Not now. Not on top of everything else. Her pride was in tatters and she still reeled from his onslaught on her senses.

Finally he moved, covering the distance between them with a few long-legged strides. He paused in front of her, head inclined towards hers, as if trying to catch her eye.

Stubbornly she resisted. She wasn't a masochist.

The masculine scents of musk and spice tickled her nostrils, and Antonia panicked as a bolt of desire shot through her. She locked her knees to steady herself, waiting.

'As for my proposition—'

'I hope you don't expect me to thank you for that!' She spoke through gritted teeth.

'The offer still stands. For a limited time.' He paused, probably waiting for her to query him or look at him, or, Heaven help her, beg for another of his kisses.

'The suite is paid for till the end of the week. You have two days before you have to vacate. I'll be back then for my money. You can give me your answer at the same time.'

Then he was gone, striding off down the corridor.

Antonia was still trying to come up with a smart rejoinder, something that would put him in his place, when she finally remembered to shut the door.

The problem was she didn't think anything she said *could* cut him down to size. His ego was so massive, his assurance so ingrained, that her feeble ripostes had no impact at all.

His proposition was pure insult. Had he realised how demeaning it was when he'd proposed such an arrangement? Or did he simply not care?

Her pride revolted. More, she felt sullied. She'd been surrounded for so long by people who cared more for their material possessions, their status and having a good time than about fidelity and love. She'd seen too much of the seamier side of life at resorts like this, travelling with small exclusive travel groups.

Her parents' marriage had been like a beacon shining above the dross. The love they'd shared had been wonderful. Long ago she'd vowed to follow their example, to give herself only to the man she loved.

She'd made one youthful mistake. A painful error of judgement that had torn at her self-esteem and her heart. But she'd recovered, all the more determined to hold out for her dream. No second best for her.

Rafe Benton had picked the wrong woman for his plans.

Two days. He had a nerve! He probably expected her to welcome him with open arms just because he kissed like an angel. No, make that a demon. For all his tenderness when he'd held her, Rafe Benton was far too ruthless and sexually experienced to masquerade as a celestial being.

Antonia was totally out of her depth with him.

That was why it was imperative she find a way to cover her father's debt and get out of here. *Quickly*.

Where could she get a significant amount of cash in just two days?

A few hours later Antonia sat in the hotel lounge, pouring tea. Hopefully the steaming brew would warm her. The flash of fury she'd experienced confronting Rafe Benton, the raw anger and—she hated to admit it—the shameful flush of feminine response to his devastating kiss, had long since seeped away.

The creeping numbness of desolation was back, icing up her body and freezing her attempts to think her way out of her problems. A detailed account of money owing had arrived within an hour of Rafe Benton's departure. It confirmed what she'd guessed. She couldn't meet the debt.

She'd contacted her bank, and some other financial institutions, but with no success. Her seasonal work and lack of assets made her a bad risk. She needed another solution—fast.

At worst she'd brazen it out and insist on a schedule of payments. She refused to countenance his proposition.

Antonia was exhausted, her mind turning fruitlessly in well-worn grooves. Despite her efforts to concentrate, she kept circling back to the accident. If only she'd been driving…

It was a relief when her mobile phone rang, dragging her back to the present.

'Antonia? It's Emma.'

'Emma!' Antonia sank back in her chair. What she needed right now was someone to talk to. Her friend Emma had perfect timing. 'It's great to hear your voice.'

'How are you doing?'

She grimaced. 'I'm holding up.'

'I'm sorry I couldn't make it to the funeral. I—'

'Please, don't apologise again. Honestly, no one

could expect you to fly out here. You're incredibly busy at the moment. Anyway, I'd rather spend time with you when I get back to England.' Antonia shivered. She never wanted to come back to this place again. 'In the meantime, it's so good to talk to you.'

'Yes. I… We need to talk.' Something about Emma's tone jarred, and Antonia straightened in her seat, the back of her neck prickling in foreboding.

'Is something wrong?' Suddenly this didn't sound like a catch-up chat.

'Yes. Yes, there is.' Emma paused so long Antonia felt the hairs rise on her nape. 'I'm so sorry. You don't need this right now, Antonia, but I can't think what else to do. I'd never forgive myself if I didn't tell you and then…'

'Emma, please. The tension is killing me.'

'Sorry. I just… It's about your father.'

'My dad?' Antonia frowned.

'Yes.' Emma dragged in a deep breath, clearly audible over the line. 'Someone recently withdrew money from one of the Foundation accounts. A lot of money.'

Antonia frowned. What did Emma's work at the Claudia Benzoni Foundation have to do with her father? The Foundation had grown into a significant enterprise, assisting sufferers worldwide and funding medical research. Her father had worked tirelessly to raise money for it. He'd been a contributor, not a beneficiary.

'I'm sorry, Emma. I don't understand.'

'The money is still missing.' Emma's sombre tone set warning bells ringing.

'What do you mean, missing?'

'I mean the withdrawals were unauthorised—totally irregular. They were made using your father's access code.'

Antonia froze, her cup halfway to her lips.

'Antonia? Are you there?'

'I'm here.' Slowly she leaned forward and put her cup on the table. Her hand was unsteady and tea sloshed into the saucer. 'Withdrawals? Plural?'

'Yes. Until eight days ago someone was systematically milking the account.'

Someone using her father's access code.

'You think my father took it.' It wasn't a question. The silence on the line told her exactly what Emma thought.

Yet the idea was absurd. The charity was all that had brought her father back from the brink of grief-stricken self-destruction all those years ago. Despite his conspicuous bonhomie and his avid enjoyment of the good things in life, there were only two things that had kept him going: his love for her and the prospect of saving others from the disease that had snatched away his wife.

'I'm just telling you what I know. The money is

gone. I've checked and triple-checked, but there's no mistake. I don't suppose your father…?'

'No! No, he didn't. He wouldn't.' But even as she said it Antonia remembered his reckless expenditure recently, his mood swings and heightened extravagance.

Desperately she shook her head. It wasn't true. No matter how depressed he'd been—and his recent behaviour had surely been a symptom of depression over his rapidly declining health—Gavin Malleson had been an honest man.

It was unthinkable that he'd steal from the one thing that had given his life purpose.

'There has to be another explanation.'

'Of course there is,' Emma said, just a shade too brightly. 'I thought maybe you'd have some idea of what might have happened. Your father didn't mention anything?'

'No. No, he didn't.' Antonia bit her lip against a traitorous wobble. What on earth was going on?

'How much money is missing?' she asked at last.

Her eyes rounded as Emma named an enormous sum.

'You're kidding!'

'I wish. An amount like this won't be overlooked, and there's an audit coming up.'

Antonia's blood froze. 'How soon?'

'In three days. And then there'll be hell to pay.' Emma sounded almost as miserable as Antonia felt.

'You know what this will mean for the Foundation once it's public? Especially since—sorry, Antonia—it does look like your father was responsible.'

'I know,' she responded in a cracked voice.

A few years ago a scandal had rocked another major aid agency with stories of officials skimming money. The allegations of corruption had been unfounded, though there had been sloppy management practices. But the damage had been done. The agency had lost the public's trust and six months later it had closed.

'Even though Dad is dead, the damage would be irreversible,' she whispered.

Gavin had been the Foundation's public face, and the press would lose no time digging up dirt—like his youthful reputation as a profligate high spender. They'd crucify his character, ignoring all the good he'd done later. The public would wonder how long he'd been skimming money.

'The Foundation would be permanently tainted. It might even fold, if it lost the public's trust.'

Antonia's body was rigid with horror as the implications sank in. Her father's reputation in his youth had been appalling. His parents had even disowned him. He'd only found stability when he married. But his attempts as an entrepreneur had failed when his wife died. Since then he'd lived off the annuity his family had settled on him years before. The press would have a field day digging that up, and if word leaked about his recent debts…

* * *

Antonia clicked the lock on the door to her suite and tottered across the room, sliding in a boneless huddle into a corner of the nearest sofa.

She was weak from the force of her nausea. She'd been comprehensively sick in the privacy of the ladies' toilets downstairs as soon as she'd ended the call from Emma. She lifted her knees, wrapping her arms round her legs, hugging tight, as if she could stop the shudders that racked her.

The world had gone mad!

First Rafe Benton, with his outrageous proposition. That had been preposterous, horrendous.

But now it wasn't just debts she had to deal with.

She'd racked her brain to find some plausible explanation for the missing funds. She and Emma had concocted a range of scenarios to account for the withdrawals, each more implausible than the last.

And all the while, despite her obstinate denials, Antonia had harboured a seed of…doubt.

She felt disloyal admitting it. But no matter how hard she tried she couldn't ignore her father's recent erratic behaviour. The extravagant spending. And the fact that the withdrawals had stopped just before her father's death.

No! It wasn't possible! She refused to believe it.

Antonia rocked back and forth, trying to find comfort in the rhythmic motion.

Whatever it took, she had to protect her father's reputation and the wonderful work he'd done. She owed it to him, and to her mother. This was all she had left of them.

The difficulty was, protecting their memories would need far more than a simple belief in her father's honesty. She grimaced and pressed her forehead down against her knees. A few hours ago she'd thought things were bad. She hadn't known the meaning of the word!

Antonia dragged in a deep, shuddering breath. She needed a plan. There must be *something* she could do.

If she could raise the money somehow, then she could cover the charity's loss until the real culprit could be identified.

She needed time to prove her father's innocence. Nothing else mattered. But that meant getting her hands on a small fortune and depositing it with the Foundation before the audit in three days' time.

She had no collateral for a loan.

She had no prospects.

She had an impossible deadline.

How far was she willing to go to save her family name and her dad's reputation? Far enough to accept Rafe Benton's proposition?

Surely she wasn't seriously considering it?

Yet the more her tired, frantic brain searched for solutions, the more quickly she came back to him.

Could she become a mistress? A paid lover for six months to a man whose arrogance and brash ruthlessness raised her hackles? But whose touch, whose kisses, unravelled her?

Whose money she could use to protect her family.

Antonia remembered the searing intensity of his gaze just before he'd kissed her, the unprecedented way she'd responded to him. Instinctively she understood he was far more dangerous than any man she'd ever encountered.

What on earth was she going to do?

CHAPTER FOUR

RAFE stared out of the café window, his espresso untouched, his thoughts fixed again on Antonia Malleson.

Despite her desperate rearguard act, trying to appear unmoved by their kiss, Rafe hadn't been fooled. She'd come alive in his arms as only a truly aroused woman could. The passion between them had accelerated from tentative to dangerously combustible as soon as he'd breached her defences and she'd given up fighting.

The woman packed a hell of a punch. His body was tight, alert at the memory of how she'd felt against him.

Yet she'd pretended she'd felt nothing. Was it pride? He'd shown no finesse, had been almost brutal as he'd told her what he wanted. His previous lovers would have been appalled. But this was different. This woman was one of his father's set, high-living and callous. She was no innocent. Not after the way she'd encouraged his father.

She'd looked down her elegant nose at Rafe as if

he'd slid out from under a rock. As if she wasn't used to mixing with anyone who called a spade a spade.

Or as if she was hiding pain.

Where had that thought come from? He frowned. When he'd held her close and tasted her honey-sweetness he'd almost believed he read vulnerability in her face and in the tightly coiled tension of her slim frame.

He dismissed the idea.

Maybe she was embarrassed at not having the cash to cover her accommodation. Dexter must be feeling the pinch already, since he hadn't bailed her out of debt. But money couldn't be a long-term problem for her. She obviously had an allowance that kept her, while others had to work for a crust. No doubt her lovers kept her supplied with luxuries.

Yet, despite all that, Antonia Malleson intrigued him as no other woman had. He rubbed his hand over his jaw.

He needed to remember she was a means to an end. A very beautiful, very tempting means to an end. White hot energy blasted through him as he thought of his mission. Of the scheme he'd put in motion since his mother's death.

As a kid, he hadn't wanted to know the father who'd rejected him before he was born. But the more he'd learned, the more inevitable it had become that there'd be a reckoning with his father one day. Now that day had arrived.

His father: Stuart Dexter. Wheeler-dealer, born

with a silver spoon in his mouth. Only Dexter was no example of British *noblesse oblige*. He was selfish to the bone. He'd bartered his family name for a fortune when he'd married. Right after he'd seduced Lillian Benton, his PA, then chucked her out, with no references and no money to help raise their child.

Dexter had expected her to have an abortion. When she'd refused he'd turned his back, threatening legal action for harassment if she tried to see him again.

That was the sort of man Rafe had for a father.

The knowledge ate into him like acid.

Even so, Rafe could have ignored Dexter—except that he'd done far more. He'd all but destroyed Lillian Benton.

Memories of his mother's face, ravaged and gaunt, haunted Rafe still. His fists clenched as he thought of the damning correspondence he'd found in her papers.

Despite the comforts he'd been able to give her at the end, when his hard work and determination had paid off so spectacularly, Rafe knew Dexter was to blame for what had gone before. *That* was unforgivable.

Ironically, it was his father who had created the opportunity for revenge. He'd made contact, proposing a joint venture. His own company was short of the ready and he wanted Rafe's money, Rafe's expertise, to help him cash in on an opportunity that would pull him out of strife.

He hadn't even bothered to find the connection between Rafe and the woman he'd seduced and then destroyed.

Rafe shoved his coffee away and stood up, too restless to sit. He grabbed his coat and stepped into the street.

A sense of rightness, of satisfaction, settled deep in his chest as he reviewed his plans. It was his duty to put an end to his father's destructive activities. To make him pay for the damage he'd done to Rafe's mother and so many other innocent people. A *family* duty.

Dexter's empire was rocky from too many dubious investments and sheer extravagance. Six months would do it. Rafe had entrusted most of his own business to hand-picked deputies while he devoted himself to the long overdue task of making Stuart Dexter pay.

His father had two weaknesses: money and women. They'd be the key to his revenge.

Shoving his hands in his pockets, Rafe turned down the street, head bent against the chill wind.

When their business was concluded Dexter would be broke and broken, his bank account empty and his ego destroyed. What gorgeous young woman would have him once he was skint?

The *coup de grâce* would be possessing the woman his father wanted so badly. His current obsession: Antonia Malleson. Rafe would make damned sure that at every party Dexter went to, every function, there she'd be. Close, but always out of reach. Another, richer man's possession.

Rafe's mistress. How sweet the satisfaction when the old man learned she'd rejected him for his own son.

It had been so simple. A phone call from his London office had sent Dexter high-tailing it back there, eager to begin discussions on their joint venture. Since then Dexter had been incommunicado, spending the last few days in meetings he assumed would pave the way to his financial salvation.

With Dexter unavailable to help her, Antonia wouldn't be able to find the cash she owed. She didn't have the resources to withstand Rafe, and the prospect of tapping into his wealth would be irresistible. He'd allowed her time to stew on her decision, but he knew her answer already. He'd left her no alternative. He had her exactly where he wanted her.

Anticipation danced in his blood.

Rafe halted in front of her hotel. It was time to secure the woman who'd make his vengeance complete.

She unlatched the door at his first knock. He'd give her that much: she didn't try to hide.

As the door swung open he felt it again. That surge of power roaring out from his belly, up through his chest, energising his whole body. He looked down into her smooth Madonna face and *knew*. This wasn't just about revenge. Not solely about his plans to bring down his father.

He wanted Antonia Malleson. Wanted her so fiercely the knowledge pounded through him with every pulse of his blood. Even if she hadn't been Stuart Dexter's current fixation, the perfect tool in Rafe's scheme, he'd want her.

With her guarded brown eyes, her mouth a tight line, her hair scraped into a severe knot and her face wiped clear of emotion, she looked cold and unwelcoming. Yet she was sexier than any woman he could remember. The sizzle of connection as their eyes met sent a jag of heat through him.

How convenient that personal inclination and duty should coalesce in this way.

This was going to be a real pleasure. *His* pleasure.

His gaze flitted down, taking in the high-necked shirt, her jacket, tailored trousers and high heels. She was dressed for business.

Yet the formal clothes didn't conceal the superb length of those slim legs, the curves in all the right places. And more. The inner strength that proclaimed she'd be no push-over but a challenge for any man who took her on.

The combination was tantalising. The touch-me-not air and the seductress body. His blood pumped faster.

He imagined peeling each garment from her till she was nude—all except for those high heels. A flash of pure need rocketed through him, tightening his groin.

'Hello, Antonia.'

'Mr Benton.' She nodded her head and stood back reluctantly to let him enter.

Antonia was glad she had hold of the doorknob. The rumbling caress of his deep voice saying her name made her knees rock. And she was already shaky from the impact of his powerful presence.

She'd screwed up her courage, knowing she had to face him. And still she hadn't been prepared. She'd hoped her reaction to him that first time had been some weird anomaly, brought on by shock and grief.

As she'd looked up into his searingly bright eyes her heart had sunk. It had been no fluke. Even knowing the sort of man he was—one who bought women for his convenience—she couldn't deny her instant physical response to him.

She tried to despise him. But, arrogant as he was, it wasn't contempt she felt.

'So formal, *Ms Malleson*?'

He stopped far too close to her, lingering less than an arm's length away in the vestibule.

She turned and glanced in his direction, careful not to meet his eyes.

'You're here on business, Mr Benton.' She drew a slow breath. 'I reserve my first name for my friends.' Ignoring the way he stilled at her taunt, she gestured to the sofas grouped in the sitting room. 'Please, take a seat.'

Then she turned away, grateful to have her back to him as she fumbled with the doorknob, her palm suddenly slippery and her fingers unsteady.

How was she going to get through this?

She still didn't have an answer. She'd spent the last two nights sleepless. There'd been long, blank periods of grief, when she'd stared dry-eyed and wondered if she'd ever feel whole again. In between she'd grappled with the impossible calculation of the money she needed and the irreparable damage that would be done if she didn't restore it. Damage to her father's name, her mother's charity and to the innocent victims relying on the Foundation.

'Aren't you going to join me?'

She felt his words like a stroke of heat down her spine. Slowly she turned and forced herself to walk into the sitting room. Anxiety knotted her stomach and anger knitted her brow. How dared he sit there, calm as could be?

'Would you like coffee, tea?' Anything to delay the moment of reckoning.

'No, thank you.' Was that amusement in his lazy tone?

'Or something else? Some other drink,' she added quickly, when she saw the speculation in his eyes.

He lolled in his seat, completely at ease, but his gaze was intent. On *her*. Antonia felt like some prized possession up for auction, displayed on a stand for bidders to view. It nauseated her.

Her careful dressing this morning hadn't helped at all. The high heels brought her closer to his height, but that just meant she'd got the full force of his intense gaze when she'd swung open the door. The impact had punched the air from her lungs. Nor did it matter how many layers she wore. She still felt vulnerable with this man.

'I don't want anything.'

He paused long enough for her to remember to exhale, then suck in some more oxygen.

'I'm here for your answer.'

Antonia nodded, and abruptly she was sitting on the sofa opposite him. Her knees had given way. She hoped for her dignity's sake he hadn't guessed how her legs had crumpled.

She spread her hands flat on the leather beside her, trying to anchor herself, the better to fight the trembling weakness that threatened to devour her. It was more than a week since the day her world had rocked off its axis. She had to face the future, no matter how unpalatable. She had a duty to her father's memory. A responsibility.

'You've considered my proposal?'

A flash of sour gallows humour snagged her. It was hardly a proposal. That sounded so respectable—like a promise of marriage. This was definitely a *proposition*, with every sordid nuance the word could convey.

'Yes, I've considered it.' She firmed her lips, horrified at the sound of her voice, raw and unsteady. She cleared her throat and looked at the bright abstract painting on the wall behind him. Anything rather than meet his eyes.

'And…?'

'And…'

Could she do it? Sell herself, her self-respect, her dignity? Her *body*?

No! She couldn't.

There must be another way. Something she'd overlooked. Some avenue she hadn't tried. She'd work tirelessly till she found it.

The tension locking her neck and jaw eased a fraction as she made up her mind. Relief at her decision eased her muscles and she sank back against the cushions. She still had twenty-four hours to come up with another solution—one that didn't involve giving herself to Rafe Benton.

'Did I tell you your friend Weber directed another couple of creditors my way? Rather *unsavoury* people. *Very* eager to have their debts settled.'

Fear tickled Antonia's nape as his words triggered an old memory, of menacing enforcers visiting her father years ago, after he'd gambled too freely.

'Of course,' he continued smoothly, 'you may have the resources to deal with them. And with any new matters that come to light in future.' He paused. 'No? As far as I can see, Ms Malleson, I'm your only option. And your time has just run out.'

Her shoulders sagged. Who was she kidding?

There *were* no other avenues.

Who'd believe in her father's innocence if there was a trail of debt enforcers clamouring for settlement? She needed help covering those debts, let alone dealing with the missing charity funds.

There was only one way to wipe the slate clean. To ensure that her father's reputation remained intact and her mother's charity safe. Only *she* could fix this.

Her fingers clawed into the soft leather. If only she had the courage of her convictions—

'Do you have an answer for me?'

Antonia snapped her head round at the impatient tone. She zeroed in on his cerulean eyes, hating this man with all the pent-up fear, despair and outrage that swamped her. He was a user, wielding power for his own gratification.

'Yes, I have an answer for you.' Her words were precise, coolly clipped and completely steady.

Antonia stifled the sharp pang of self-loathing that threatened her cut-glass composure. She was determined to lock away her emotions. That was the only way to deal with Rafe Benton. This man would *never* see her vulnerable. She swore it to herself. Whatever happened, she'd be strong.

She tilted her chin up and sent him the sort of chilly stare she'd seen so many wealthy women bestow on insignificant beings like hapless tour guides.

'I accept your offer.'

CHAPTER FIVE

RAFE'S surge of elation was so great he had to smother the smile tugging at his lips.

He had her.

Antonia Malleson had been a constant distraction. He'd been busy communicating with his deputies in Australia and London. But instead of its usual total focus on commercial challenges, his mind had wandered far too often. This woman had disrupted his hectic daytime schedule just as she'd wreaked havoc with his nights.

Now that was over.

He could have what he so desired. The sexy Ms Malleson and the perfect completion of his revenge on Stuart Dexter.

Adrenaline pulsed through his blood. Eagerness.

Never had a woman disturbed him so much. It was amazing, given how little time he'd spent with her. He looked forward to seeing if all her kisses were so incendiary. And more. His blood heated as his mind raced at a vision of her naked in his bed.

He strove to remind himself that the pleasure he felt was because he'd turned the tables on this grasping beauty, making her fit *his* scheme.

'But I have a condition.'

She crossed one leg over another, the pull of dark fabric emphasising the saucy curve of her hip and the length of her thigh.

Instantly heat flared in Rafe's belly, and he lifted his gaze to hers. If they were talking conditions, he couldn't let himself get distracted by pleasures to come.

'Yes? What is it?'

'That bonus you promised me.'

He nodded. He'd decided on the bonus after six months to ensure he had her for the whole period. He intended to parade the fact that she was *his* until the very day he closed Dexter down. Besides, he suspected it would take a full six months to have his fill of her.

'What about it?'

'I want double and I want it up-front.'

His brows rose. She had to be kidding. He'd already agreed to waive her substantial debts. How much did she think she was worth?

Rafe had never paid for a woman in his life. If not for these peculiar circumstances, he'd never have considered it. He had no knowledge of the usual fee structure, but surely the glossy, well-kept women he'd met with their older lovers didn't get such a large bonus?

'Why should I pay you that kind of money?'

She shrugged, her lips softening in the tiniest hint of a pout that made his mouth dry.

'If you want me to agree, that's what it'll cost you.'

'And what do I get for the extra money?'

Her fine brows arched, her dark eyes widening in a show of condescension that would have done a duchess proud.

An insistent voice inside urged him to agree to her terms. Six months with her would be worth every penny.

For the sake of his revenge, of course.

'I would live as your…mistress for six months.' She spoke calmly, her voice uninflected, as if she were selling a commodity, not herself.

No doubt she had more experience of these arrangements than he did. The realisation brought a twist of sharp sensation to his chest.

'What? No extra perks? No *special* treatment?'

Cool morphed to glacial in a look that should have frozen him to the spot. Obviously his mistress-to-be wasn't impressed. Perhaps she intended to charge by the hour for anything else? Negotiating with her was like taking on a savvy, stony-faced business competitor.

Avidly, Rafe wondered how long it would take to heat her blood to a point where passion took over from mercenary instincts. This woman excited him as no other.

'I'll be your mistress for the period you stipulated. Isn't that what you wanted?'

Of course it was. Though *want* was too bland a word. If she changed her mind, how would he satisfy this...craving?

'You'll live with me in *every* sense? Do as I wish?'

For a moment something flickered in her eyes, something he couldn't define, then she nodded her head abruptly. 'Within reason.'

'Oh, I'm always *reasonable*, Antonia.'

He watched her stiffen at the use of her name. That would have to end.

'All right. I'll give you double what I promised you, spread out in monthly payments—'

'No!'

He watched, fascinated, as a hint of colour appeared on her high cheekbones. It made him wonder how she'd look flushed from lovemaking.

Soon he'd know.

'No?'

She shook her head. 'That won't do. I want payment up-front. Before I leave here.'

'That's asking a lot, don't you think?'

'What? And you're not asking a lot from me?' Her nostrils flared in disdain and her lips primmed. He remembered the taste of her, like honey and raw desire in his mouth. The softness of her hair to his touch. The heat of her body against his.

He'd certainly make sure he got his money's worth out of this transaction—one way or another.

'Fine. Give me your bank details and I'll have the money transferred immediately. Seventy five percent now. Twenty five percent at the end of our arrangement.'

She stilled. He could almost hear her quick mental calculations. Then she reached for her purse and took out a card. He watched her note down the account number. Her movements were controlled, brisk and definite. Almost jerky.

Stress? Could it be?

'You're sure about this?' he found himself asking, amazed at the words emerging from his mouth. It wasn't like him to stymie his own deal.

'Sure that I want that extra payment?' Her lips tilted up in a brittle smile and she laughed—a short tinkle of sound that reminded him, absurdly, of breaking glass. 'Oh, yes, I'm sure. No up-front payment, no deal.'

She leaned over the table towards him, holding out a piece of paper with her account details.

Rafe sat forward and claimed her hand with his own. Her eyes widened and her mouth sagged open a little. At her wrist he felt the flutter of her pulse.

Not so assured, then. Interesting. Antonia Malleson was fast becoming an enigma he wanted to solve.

Or perhaps *unwrap* was a better word.

He encircled her hand, enjoying the feel of her smooth skin, her delicate bones within his grasp.

'I have a condition too,' he murmured, enjoying the immediate flare of consternation in her dark eyes. 'We'll use first names. I refuse to be called "Mr Benton" by my mistress. And I'm sure there'll be times when "Antonia" is more appropriate than "Ms Malleson".'

Colour suffused her cheeks. With her pale gold skin tones it brought a healthy glow to a face that had been too pale, he realised.

The pulse beneath his hand jumped, and he knew they were thinking of the same thing. The pair of them together in bed. This time he did smile, as heady anticipation coursed through his bloodstream.

'First names it is. Now, would you mind releasing my hand? It's uncomfortable, leaning across like this.'

'Of course.' He let her go and took the all-important bank details. Then he stood and walked around to where she sat. 'Shall we seal the arrangement with a celebratory kiss?' That would do for starters.

His words were barely out when she shot to her feet, glaring up at him almost belligerently.

'No. No celebrations until the money comes through.'

Stunned, Rafe stared down at her. Did she expect him to renege on his promise? He frowned. More proof that she'd been hanging around with the wrong sort of men.

'I mean it!'

'Okay.' He raised his hands in a gesture of placation, surprised to hear a note that sounded like panic in her voice. Carefully he scrutinised her, but he couldn't read a thing. That severe expression of calm was back in place, like a mask hiding whatever went on in her mind.

'I'll collect you in the morning, so you'll need to be ready to leave.'

'How long before I get my money?' she countered.

Her avaricious streak was a mile wide. She didn't even bother to hide it. Strange how the idea disappointed him. Yet if she'd been a different sort of woman she wouldn't have agreed to his proposition.

'Within the hour.'

She paused a minute, glancing at her watch. Was she wondering if she had time for some last-minute shopping with his money before she packed?

'Yes. I can be ready.'

'No questions about where we're going?' Surely she'd have to choose what to pack and what to send home?

She shook her head. 'No.'

Rafe narrowed his eyes. She had to be the most uncommunicative woman he'd ever met. And the least curious.

That made her doubly intriguing.

Silently she stood, again looking at something over his shoulder. Whatever it was, it was damned fascinating. Rafe frowned. He'd have thought *he'd* be more interesting to her than some brightly daubed painting. After all, he was the man who'd just bought her for half a year.

The thought cheered him.

'I'll see you at eight sharp, Antonia.'

'I'll meet you in the foyer, Mr Benton.'

He raised a brow. 'We agreed to first names.'

'So we did.' She inclined her head in a regal gesture. 'The agreement will apply *after* you make the payment.'

Vixen! For a moment he was tempted to ignore her supercilious air, tug her into his arms and teach her just who was in control in this relationship.

No one walked over Rafe Benton. He was well past the age of being dictated to. But a streak of selfish enjoyment made him hold back. Let her play her little game for now. It would make her surrender all the sweeter.

'Of course, Ms Malleson.'

He reached for her hand with his, as if to shake it. She tensed instantly, but didn't resist. At the last moment he gave in to the impulse that had gnawed at him since he'd walked into the room. The impulse to taste her again.

He took a pace forward, closing the gap between them as he raised her hand. His eyes on hers, he pressed his lips to the back of her hand and was rewarded with a tremor of response. Her pulse jumped beneath his fingers and he smiled against her skin.

Not so calm and controlled now, madam.

He turned her hand over, keeping his gaze fixed on the shadow of expression that flickered across her eyes. Slowly, oh-so-deliberately, he kissed the centre of her palm, inhaling the heady scent of her warm flesh and her soft cinnamon perfume. It surprised him, as it had two days ago. He'd expected something more sophisticated, more expensive, for a woman in her fast-living, high-spending set. Yet it suited her. It was warm, intriguing, subtly seductive. Dangerously addictive.

Her dark eyes glazed with heat, and gold sparks flared as he licked her palm, drawing the fresh, sweet taste of her into his mouth.

That was better. He felt her pulse race, a quiver of weakness ripple through her, even as his body hardened, ready for the next step towards shared pleasure.

He licked again, more slowly, enjoying the stifled sound of her hissed breath and the knowledge that she was far from immune to him.

She tried to pull her hand away. She wasn't a woman to give anything for nothing—even something as honest and straightforward as mutual passion. For a moment longer he held her hand captive, making sure she understood that the power rested with him. Then he let her fingers slide free.

Rafe straightened, watching the way she cradled her palm within her other hand. As if the sensations he'd evoked had burnt her. How would she react when he kissed more than her hand or her mouth?

Rafe permitted himself a small smile.

'Until tomorrow at eight, Ms Malleson. I'll look forward to commencing our arrangement.'

She made no comment as he strode across the room, opened the door and headed for the stairs.

That afternoon Antonia arranged to repay the Foundation. The transaction would look irregular, but that couldn't be helped. The main thing was that the money would be there. If there were raised brows among the auditors, surely that wouldn't affect the Foundation publicly?

Even with Rafe Benton's cash things would be tight. She'd have to sell her mother's jewellery to cover the few debts he hadn't bought up. But that was the least of her concerns. It was the missing charity funds that had kept her awake each night.

Accepting his offer had been her only choice. But it was worth it, she assured herself the following morning. This was the last thing she could do for her parents.

Antonia blinked back the prickling burn behind her eyes. Strange how emotion side-swiped her when she least expected it. If she'd been going to weep, surely that would have come at the beginning, before the funeral?

She spun away from the window. She had no time for grief. For any emotion. Not if she wanted to survive the next six months. Emotion was a luxury she couldn't afford.

In precisely five minutes she had to go downstairs and meet the man who'd bought her.

A trickle of raw fear slid down her spine and wrapped around her heart, squeezing tight. *What had she done?*

Hysteria threatened at the idea of *her* as a rich man's mistress. She, whose dream wasn't wealth or glamour. Antonia had seen the ultra-rich from far too close. Generally she didn't like what she saw.

She was the cuckoo in the nest. Her dreams were mundane: a home, rather than a succession of hotels. A sense of belonging, a man who'd love her, a family of her own. To study art, then find a job that would give her the security she'd never had because of her dad's wandering lifestyle. She could have left him and pursued her own dreams. But these last few years she'd been so worried about him that she'd put her dreams on hold.

She picked up her bag with a shaking hand and cast a final glance around the room. She'd known grief and despair here, loss and marrow-deep pain, but this place marked the end of her old life.

Sucking in a deep breath, she walked out through the door, closing it with a click that sounded abnormally loud in the hushed stillness. The lift was deserted except for the tall woman with dark hair who stared at her from the mirror on the back wall. One glance at those empty eyes and she turned abruptly to punch the button for the ground floor.

So what if she didn't recognise herself? Wasn't that better? Maybe she could pretend this was happening to someone else, not her?

The doors slid open and she stepped out. The first thing she saw was him.

Rafe Benton looked tall and devilish all in black: trousers, pullover and long coat. His dark hair was combed severely back from his broad forehead. He didn't notice her and she scanned his profile, the cut of his jaw, the angle of his cheekbone and the strong slant of his nose. They made up a formidable whole, compelling rather than handsome.

No hope that he'd changed his mind.

Antonia faltered as the urge to flee caught her. Then his eyes met hers. Electric-blue fire blasted across the space between them and she knew there was no escape.

Wherever she went he'd come after her. There was no mistaking the determination in that face. The flash of possessiveness in those eyes. She repressed a tremor of foreboding as heat licked her skin.

Besides, she'd given her word, taken his money. No one would ever again accuse a Malleson of dishonesty.

She watched his well-shaped mouth curl at the corners. He had a tantalising half-smile most women would find devastating, especially when teamed with those vibrantly blue eyes.

It was all she could do to walk towards him, one foot carefully in front of the other. He held her gaze through every slow, agonising step.

On the periphery of her vision she saw other people in the foyer. Yet the sound of them was muted, drowned out by the heavy pulsing silence between her and Rafe Benton.

'Hello, Antonia.' His smile widened a fraction, as if he relished the sound of her name.

For an instant she baulked. But resistance was pointless.

'Hello…Rafe.' Her voice sounded calm. Yet her heart plummeted as she swallowed the sour taste of capitulation and self-contempt. She'd just crossed an invisible boundary, implicitly accepting his terms. She'd gone from free woman to paid consort.

She'd left her self-respect behind.

Rafe watched her lips shape his name and his satisfaction grew. It was good to see her behaving reasonably. After paying through the nose for her co-operation he wouldn't brook any nonsense.

He felt a punch of desire. She had such a gorgeous mouth. Such soft lips. Perfect. He enjoyed the way she said his name, too, with her neat British accent.

He considered planting a swift kiss on her mouth, a gesture of possession and of need. But he decided against it. He was aware of the other guests, of staff watching them curiously. No. When he kissed her it would be in private, where he could enjoy her sensuality to the full.

'I'm glad to see you're punctual. I'm not a man who appreciates being kept waiting.'

Her look told him she understood that he was talking about more than being in time for a rendezvous. Good.

'Where's your luggage?' He was eager to leave.

'Over there.' She pointed to two suitcases by the concierge's desk.

'That's it?' From his experience of women, there had to be more. These were too modest. 'You've sent the rest of your things home?'

When she didn't answer, he shrugged. He wasn't interested in her luggage. Pleasure stirred at the knowledge she was his. He could put his plans into action.

He turned and put his hand under her elbow, ignoring the way she froze. That would stop soon. Soon she'd be used to his touch, eager for it.

Rafe had no false modesty about his attractiveness or his ability to satisfy women. His lovers were well pleasured. So well, in fact, it was often a problem getting them to leave. He didn't doubt for an instant that Antonia would get as much satisfaction from their liaison as he intended to take.

Besides, despite the wintry reserve she wore like armour, she'd been pliant enough when he'd kissed her. The memory of her soft body melting against his, of her responding to his caresses with her lips and tongue, her hands clutching at his skull, was a clear promise of things to come. A knot of anticipation clenched in his groin.

'Come on. We have a plane to catch.'

She didn't answer, didn't even ask where they were flying, but then he'd specified he wanted a compliant mistress. Rafe had no problem with silence. It made a nice change from so many women he'd met. Like the bimbo who'd set herself to catch his attention in the bar last night. All chatter and cleavage and candyfloss between the ears. Give him an intelligent woman any day.

He glanced down at Antonia. Elegant, reserved, sexy in a way that owed nothing to silicone implants or Botox or even a dazzle of jewellery. Mind sharp as a tack. Tongue to match.

Rafe's mouth kicked up in a smile. Melting that reserve of hers was going to be pure pleasure.

Despite the luxury of his limousine, and the private jet, Antonia couldn't relax. She was too conscious of Rafe beside her, even when he turned his attention to his laptop in flight.

At least he didn't touch her, not like a man touched his mistress. But even his warm grip of her elbow, ostensibly helping her on board, his hand at the small of her back, ushering her through Customs, were enough to keep her on tenterhooks.

The trip passed quickly. She'd checked him out on the internet and she wasn't surprised. The story of his meteoric rise to success in the world of international finance hinted at someone of daunting intellect, determination and impatience. He had the spectacular wealth to make international travel smooth and easy.

Which meant they arrived at their destination far too soon. London. That was a good thing, she told herself, as they stood in the lift of a luxury apartment building. He must be here to work, which meant less time with her.

She'd worried he might take her to some exotic island where there'd be no distractions. Just him and her. All night and all day.

The idea had sent her cold with horror, and hot with something she feared might be eagerness. For she couldn't forget the way he'd kissed her. The warmth and tenderness that had somehow bypassed her guard and left her defenceless and wanting.

'Here we are. Your home for the next six months.'

He ushered her out on the top floor, straight into a massive apartment that looked as if it should be on the cover of some glossy architectural digest. Antonia had a fleeting impression of a lofty space, a vast floor of exquisite parquetry, and a view of the Thames—a perfect backdrop to expensively simple furnishings.

She barely took it in. Instead every nerve strained taut as she focused on *him*, wondering about his next move. The silence between them weighed her down.

It was fraught with unspoken expectation. Would he demand—?

'Let me take your coat.' His fingers brushed her and she stiffened, aware that at any moment his touch might grow all too personal. Heaven help her, she'd put herself in a position where she couldn't protest.

'Thank you.' Her voice was a low, grating whisper.

She was wound too tight, like a clockwork toy about to spring apart. Her heart juddered hard against her ribs and she focused on taking slow breaths as he eased her coat from her shoulders and stowed it in a nearby closet.

Then he stood before her, his eyes darkening to a shade she hadn't seen. The intensity of his expression made her breathless, nervous. Expectant. His large hand was warm against her chilled flesh as he tilted her face up. His expression was smug, his eyes alight with a blatant look of ownership that made her blood run cold.

'Alone at last.' He smiled on the words and her heart plunged.

CHAPTER SIX

WHAT had Rafe expected to find as he stared into her beautiful eyes? Bone-melting invitation? A sultry look that told him she was ready and eager for him?

He found neither. There was no welcome, either subtle or blatant. No hint of the attraction that had sparked and sizzled when they'd kissed and she'd transformed in his arms from distant to warm and willing.

Nor was there a trace of the fiery defiance he'd got such a kick out of when they clashed. She was pale, despite her golden olive complexion. There were blue smudges beneath her eyes, and weariness in the slight frown marring her brow. She looked as if she hadn't slept in days.

He hadn't noticed before, because he'd avoided looking. There'd been that first sweeping survey at the hotel, when he'd been rocked by the intensity of his pleasure at seeing her. Later he'd concentrated on work, trying to ignore his hunger for her. He refused to give in to it too soon or too completely. Rafe never gave in to weakness.

Hardly ever.

He bent his head, half expecting her to jerk away. But she stood statue-still. He brushed his lips across hers. For a moment he thought she was going to deny him, and his fingers tightened on her jaw. But her lips were pliant as he slid his mouth along hers. She accommodated him, tentatively shaping to his mouth.

Need rocketed through him as she followed his lead, met his kiss with a gentle response that was somehow more exciting than a full-on passionate embrace.

He deepened the kiss, touching her still only with his hand and his mouth. But the sensation of his tongue sliding against hers, the welcoming heat of her mouth, open for his pleasure, was undeniably erotic.

His for the taking. The knowledge was a naked flame igniting the embers of desire he'd banked down all day.

Reluctantly he pulled away, ignoring the thunder in his blood that demanded he follow through, haul her into his arms and take her to bed right now. His hands shook with the effort of restraint. Despite the clamour of his needy body, this wasn't the time.

'Welcome to your new home.' He searched for a spark of animation in her eyes. Heat to match the fire in his belly.

There was nothing. Her eyes remained blank and remote, shadowed, as if she'd withdrawn behind a wall of secrets.

That annoyed him. *He* was aware of *her* with every sense. Her enticing cinnamon-spice scent filled his nostrils. Her smooth skin was warm satin under his hand. He heard the sound of her breathing, rapid in the silence. And the taste of her, the richest, sweetest flavour in the world, lingered on his tongue, making him hungry for more.

Where had she withdrawn to? How could she be so unaffected?

Rafe was used to women dissolving at the knees when he kissed them. He frowned. It hadn't been a passionate kiss, just a foretaste of gratification to come. But surely he wasn't the only one to feel that scorch of desire? The idea was unthinkable.

'Thank you,' she said politely, as if they were total strangers. 'The apartment looks very pleasant.'

Very pleasant! Was that the best she could do? She looked utterly calm and contained, unimpressed by the obvious luxury of her surroundings. *By him.*

'And so it should be.' His tone was curt. 'It would almost have been cheaper to buy the place than to rent it for six months.'

He glanced dismissively around the room, as if the exquisite oriental rugs, the expensive and elegant furniture, meant nothing to him. Antonia wondered if he'd even noticed the painting opposite the fireplace. It looked like a Chagall, and it wasn't a print.

'If there's one thing you British know how to do, it's charge a premium rate for your bargains, isn't it?'

His laser-bright eyes pinioned her where she stood.

His expression wasn't as warm as a few moments ago, when she'd struggled to maintain some mental distance. His surprisingly tender kiss had undermined her defences and she'd barely managed to maintain her pose of uninterest.

'I only hope I won't be disappointed,' he said, clear challenge in his voice. 'When I pay top dollar I expect the best in *everything*. I don't take kindly to getting anything less than full value for my…purchases.'

Antonia stiffened, jerking her chin from his hand.

He meant *her*. She saw it in his accusing blue eyes.

He'd bought her, and now he expected her to deliver. What would he consider good value? Utter compliance? Enough sexual expertise to seduce and please a jaded appetite? Heaven help her, she wasn't equipped for this.

Nausea rose in her throat, and her skin prickled as white-hot pain encircled her forehead. Antonia swallowed hard, forcing back bile at the idea of giving herself when her emotions weren't engaged. Laying aside her pride and her natural reserve and becoming Rafe Benton's sex toy!

The idea was absurd, but she wasn't laughing. There was an aching hollow inside her. She'd given her word, taken his money. There was no going back.

'You'll also find we have a reputation for honesty in our dealings.' She forced herself to look into the bright glare of his eyes, to face down his cynicism and ignore the whimpering part of her soul that wanted to curl up in a corner and pretend this wasn't happening.

'If it's all right with you, I'd like to freshen up after the journey.' Anything to put some distance between them. If he touched her again, the consequences wouldn't bear thinking about. She'd either go up like flame in his arms, or the safety net she'd built around her feelings would be breached and she'd give in to the pain and fear that crowded so close. Either option was untenable.

'Of course.' Rafe gave a mocking bow. She didn't miss the amused tilt of his lips. 'This way.' He gestured to a wide hall. 'And I'll show you to your room.'

Her room? Was it possible she'd have her own space? Surely a mistress—?

'I prefer to sleep alone,' he said as they walked down the hall, just as if she'd voiced the question aloud. 'You'll have your own bedroom and bathroom.'

Antonia nodded, biting her lip at the edge of hysteria rising inside her. As if this sort of conversation was in any way normal. Her legs moved stiffly, her whole body taut as they approached the bedrooms.

'Here you are.' He gestured for her to precede him.

For the longest moment she hesitated. Crossing this threshold was like crossing her own personal Rubicon.

No. That had been yesterday, when she'd taken his money.

Antonia ignored his narrowed gaze and walked in.

She faltered to a stop just inside. She hadn't expected anything like this. To one side was a wall of glass, beyond that the Thames, and the rooftops of central London. Mere mortals couldn't afford vistas like this.

Yet the view barely registered. Instead she took in the room, piece by piece. A huge four-poster bed sat against one wall, each post carved to look like the trunk of a tree. At the top a criss-cross of branches supported a canopy of sheer fabric that draped to the floor. The coverlet was a fantasy of white on white embroidery, topped with plump pillows and a scattering of gold cushions.

The walls were soft ochre, a perfect foil for the timber. In front of a long set of book-lined shelves were a wing chair, with a massive ottoman, plus a sofa. There was a large cabinet that she guessed hid a television, and on another wall a medieval-style tapestry of elegant ladies gathering flowers while their beaux watched from horseback. It had the mellow look of the genuine article.

'It's beautiful,' she whispered, wishing she could think of a better description. The room was wonderful. It felt warm, welcoming, safe. A haven from the outside world.

'I'm glad you approve,' he murmured, his voice a silken skein that unravelled something deep inside her. 'I wondered if you'd prefer something more modern.'

She was aware of him behind her, of the heat of his breath on her neck. Suddenly her delight vanished.

Her gaze darted to the wide bed. This time she didn't see its whimsical fantasy. Just its size. More than big enough for two. She visualised him there, his hair dark against the pure white of the bedlinen. His tanned skin gleaming in the soft glow of the bedside lamps. His long limbs stretched out almost the full length of the bed.

And with him a woman with her mother's thick, wavy hair and dark eyes. A woman with her father's wide mouth and lanky frame. A woman who'd sold herself to keep her father's reputation and achievements safe.

The nausea hit her full force this time, and she hurried across the room to an open door. Sure enough, it was a bathroom.

She nudged the door shut and fumbled the lock closed. Then she was leaning over the sink, trembling arms braced. Her stomach was a roiling mess and acid burned her throat as she struggled to keep her last meal down.

'Antonia! Are you all right?' His voice was sharp.

Probably wondering if she was trying to renege on their deal, she thought waspishly as shudders racked her.

'I'm…fine,' she croaked, as the nausea slowly subsided. Her stomach cramped. Just as well she'd been too nervous to eat.

Eventually she felt steady enough to stand up straight. She longed to kick off her high heels, but she had so few weapons in her armoury, and the additional height gave her the illusion of strength. She was desperate enough to cling even to that hollow illusion. She rinsed her mouth, smoothed back her hair and unlocked the door.

He stood a few feet away, his expression unreadable. An article she'd read about him on the web suddenly sprang to mind. It had described him as brilliant, acute, decisive and unorthodox. He was renowned for his ability to wrong-foot competitors with daring, unexpected moves.

Uneasily Antonia wondered what he was thinking—what he saw as he watched her so closely.

'You're not well.' It wasn't a question.

She lifted her shoulders in a shrug. 'It must have been something I ate,' she lied. 'I'm all right now.'

The harsh lines around his mouth told her he doubted it.

'You need to sit down.' Without waiting for agreement, he put his arm beneath her elbow and pulled her away from the door. Panic shot through her as she thought of that luxurious bed so close, but instead he ushered her to the cushioned wing chair. Gratefully she sank into its comfort. She felt as if she'd aged decades in the last couple of weeks. Sixty-two instead of twenty-two.

'You're shaking,' he accused.

'I told you—I ate something that disagreed with me.'

He sat on the ottoman, elbows on his splayed knees as he leaned towards her. He crowded her space.

'You haven't eaten anything since we left the resort.'

She shrugged. 'I'm just...tired.'

His stare was steady, doubting. He didn't believe her. Sitting so near, the strength of his personality was a potent, palpable force. His distrust was tangible.

'Too tired for sex, you mean? Is that what this is about?'

'I...' Antonia looked away. Had he guessed how she felt? Did he have even a spark of sympathy for her situation?

'If so, you can put your mind at rest.' His tone was harsh. 'I have more important things on my mind right now.' He paused long enough to draw her gaze back to his gleaming eyes. 'Besides, given your reputation for flitting from one man to another, I'm not taking you to bed without protection. I won't run the risk of contracting whatever is doing the rounds.'

Antonia's mouth sagged in disbelief. He made her sound like some undiscriminating street walker. Someone who'd been intimate with countless strangers.

If only he knew! His just-bought mistress was hardly the experienced seductress he obviously expected.

She'd only had one serious boyfriend. Foolishly, she'd believed Peter different from the other rich guys she'd met. Until she'd discovered his idea of an exclusive relationship was ensuring his girlfriend didn't meet the women with whom he had casual sex when she wasn't around. Since then she'd only dated to stop her father fretting that she was lonely.

'Are you always this insulting to your women, Rafe?'

His eyes narrowed as he watched her convulsive swallow. Either she was the best actress he'd come across, or she really was unwell. Yet the way she said his name, in that low, throaty purr, was pure dynamite. Pale and clearly exhausted, and still she made a direct hit on his libido.

'Hardly an insult. I'm just being practical.' Though, as he took in the almost febrile glitter of her eyes and the flush staining her cheeks, Rafe knew he could have been more tactful. 'After all, this is about *your* protection as well. You don't know if I'm clean of disease either.'

'Are you?'

Rafe was surprised to feel heat flare under his skin as her gaze held his.

'Yes, I am.' He was usually very discriminating in his lovers. 'But you shouldn't take my word for it.'

'Oh, I won't.'

Rafe's jaw tightened. What was it about this woman? One minute he felt protective towards her. The next she infuriated him. For a crazy moment he'd even felt a pang of guilt, wondering if he'd been too ruthless, forcing her into this. Until he recalled that it was her own mercenary instinct, her yearning for money, that had led her here.

The only constant was his desire. And her usefulness, he reminded himself. He looked into her gorgeous face and wanted her with a need so strong it carved a hollow in his gut. A need that threatened to overcome his self-control.

Rafe surged to his feet and strode to the door. The news he'd received on the plane, that some New York negotiations had hit a snag and needed his immediate personal intervention, meant he had no time for this now. Business would surely take his mind off this woman and allow him to get his priorities right again.

'I'll leave you to settle in.'

* * *

Two mornings later Antonia checked her make-up carefully, ensuring it hid the ravages of sleepless nights before leaving her room.

She hadn't seen Rafe since their arrival in London. He'd left almost immediately afterwards on business and she'd been on tenterhooks since, wondering when he'd return. When he'd want…her.

Late last night he'd returned. She'd lain, breathing shallow and body stiff, waiting for him to enter her room. But he'd left her in peace. *For how much longer?*

Her stomach churned at the prospect of giving herself to him. Steadfastly she ignored the disquieting idea that though she didn't like Rafe, it was just possible she *did* want him. The damning memory of her capitulation when he'd kissed her made her blood tingle. She hadn't been prepared for the hungry way her body had responded to him.

No! It wasn't true. She didn't want him. She'd never be attracted to a man like that. So domineering. So willing to ride roughshod over others to get what he wanted.

So powerfully compelling.

'Antonia! Looking as lovely as ever.'

She had a fleeting impression of glinting blue eyes and then strong arms swept her up, pulling her close. His heat, the intense masculine scent of his skin, surrounded her as he delved into her mouth, staking his ownership with no preliminaries, no hesitation.

Her head reeled from the sudden sensual onslaught, and she grasped at his shoulders as her knees weakened. He moulded her body against his and she didn't have time to construct any defences. Horrified, she felt a flicker of delight at the way they fitted together, as if this was what she'd missed these last sleepless nights.

He pulled away abruptly, just as she absorbed the taste of him on her tongue, recognised its familiarity. She clung to him a fraction too long—finding her balance, she assured herself. But she couldn't miss the satisfaction in his eyes as he stood back and surveyed her.

His eyes crinkled at the corners and his lips quirked up in a half-smile that was both intimate and devastating.

'I see you missed me too, sweetheart,' he murmured.

'I—' A finger on her lips stilled her denial.

'No, don't spoil the illusion.' For a long moment his gaze held hers and inexplicable warmth traced her body.

'You've got your bag? Good. Come on. I have an early meeting and I want your company on the way.'

'But I can't. I haven't—'

'No buts, Antonia.' He tucked her arm in his and strode to the lift, pulling her with him. 'A man likes his mistress to be amenable. I'm sure you can manage it. Just think of all that lovely money in your bank account.'

His words stiffened her spine. All traces of the strange bone-melting sensation that had so weakened her during his kiss bled away. She stood ramrod-straight beside him in the lift, staring blankly at the control console.

'Not going to ask me where I've been, sweet-heart?'

She hated that lazy drawl, the way it curled insidiously deep inside her despite his obvious sarcasm.

'I'm sure you'll tell me if you want to.'

The lift doors opened and she moved to slip her arm free. But there was no escape. He simply snagged her close, his body solid and intimidatingly large beside her.

'Not happy this morning, Antonia?'

'I'm fine.' What did he want her to say? That she enjoyed being treated as a chattel, her movements circumscribed by his whims?

Silently he led her out to a waiting limousine. When they were inside, cut off from the driver by a privacy screen, Rafe turned those laser-bright eyes on her.

'All right, Antonia. What's your problem?'

Her problem? He had to be kidding.

'If you're not happy with our arrangement then say so *now*. I didn't force you into accepting my more than generous offer.' He crossed his arms over his deep chest as he spoke, the picture of male power and annoyance.

Despite herself Antonia felt a thrill of pleasure at

having unwittingly provoked him. No, that was too dangerous. Who knew what Rafe Benton would do if pushed too far?

'I refuse to put up with a woman who sulks and pouts her way through a relationship.'

'I—'

'I paid good money for the pleasure of your company, Antonia. And I expect more than this in return.'

Yes, master. Whatever you say, master.

Antonia took refuge in bitter anger. Reality was too unpalatable—for he *had* bought her. She'd made the choice to accept his offer. No matter that she'd been desperate.

'Unless you'd prefer to pay back my cash advance?'

Instantly her defiance waned. That was one thing she simply couldn't do. She'd already spent his precious cash.

'Perhaps you'd better spell out exactly what it is you require,' she said, when she'd found her voice.

Rafe's brows rose as if in astonishment.

'I mean…' she fought down a blush '…when we're not…'

'Making love?' Those two words, uttered in his deep, sultry voice, drew every muscle tight. In revulsion, she assured herself. Not excitement.

'Yes,' she whispered, her throat constricting.

'It's simple, Antonia.' His voice was grim. 'Given the small fortune I've paid for the *pleasure* of your company, you'll be with me whenever I want you from this moment on.'

She stared at him, conscious of the way the wide back seat seemed to shrink as his gaze clashed and meshed with hers. Of how close he was to her. And of the way her pulse raced at the possessive gleam in his eyes.

'You're mine—bought and paid for.' His voice dropped a notch. The sound of it, like a rumbling purr, made her skin prickle with gooseflesh and her breath stop. 'You'd do well to remember that.'

A wave of energy pulsed between them as his words sank in. Owner and chattel. Man and mistress. Clearly there was no difference in his mind, nor any way out. Antonia absorbed the blow as she had so many others. She told herself she could weather this as she had everything else.

By the end of summer she'd be free. Her own woman. She could take up the career she'd wanted for so long but had delayed in order to take care of her father. She'd start afresh, build a safe, secure life for herself.

'Of course, Rafe.' She paused on his name, her throat closing reflexively, but she forced the word out. Surely it would become easier with time? 'So what did you have in mind next?' She prayed that he couldn't hear the trepidation in her voice.

For a long time he studied her, as if probing for secrets. It was unnerving. He shouldn't be interested in her secrets. He only wanted physical gratification, and the titillating knowledge that she was at his beck and call.

The idea was degrading. But perhaps it offered a way out. If she focused on complying with his whims perhaps she could ignore the welter of emotions that threatened to destroy her composure. If she could divorce her feelings from the need to act the part of his woman, *bought and paid for*, she might just be able to get through this.

'Next I have business to attend to. So you'll have to amuse yourself for the day.' He paused. Was he expecting her to complain? It was all she could do not to grin her relief at the reprieve.

'But tonight we'll go out. We'll be attending a series of engagements from now on. Receptions, dinners and balls. I'll expect you to be *close* at my side for every one.' His brows arrowed into a frown as if he dared her to argue. 'I want an attentive companion—understood?'

'Understood.' She'd hang on his every word.

'One who smiles occasionally.'

She could manage that. Especially if they were at a crowded reception where she wouldn't be caught in the illusion that there was no one but the pair of them in the whole world. When he stared at her so intensely, like now, everything else faded away. It unnerved her.

'No flinching when I put my arm around you. No acting like a scalded cat whenever I touch you.' He was remembering her reaction as he'd marched her to the limousine. Every time he touched her she stiffened.

He was a very tactile man. She'd noticed the way his hand strayed so often to the small of her back, ushering her through a door or into a vehicle. He'd take her arm in his and match his long-legged stride to hers. And each time she'd freeze, horrified at the splintering shards of unwanted awareness arrowing through her at the contact.

She'd wondered whether it was just in his nature to draw close, or if it was an unspoken sign of ownership. For a man so controlled, so calculating, there was a disturbingly sensuous streak to Rafe Benton. Her guess was that he simply enjoyed physical contact. The idea had banished sleep as she tossed in her bed, imagining how it would feel to have those large hands, that body, on hers.

'Antonia?' His tone was impatient.

'Of course,' she murmured. 'No flinching.'

His eyes narrowed, as if he suspected sarcasm.

'I've already mentioned attentiveness,' he warned.

Just as well he had no idea she'd been distracted by thoughts of his touch. His ego would balloon phenomenally if he knew.

'I'll be attentive,' she assured him.

His muffled sigh was the only response. Masculine impatience barely stifled.

'And I want you to look glamorous. No fading into the background.' He dropped his gaze to her grey trousers and jacket, her low-heeled shoes, and his frown deepened.

No doubt he'd want to show off his new trophy. His taste was probably for showy ostentation.

'How formal are these receptions we're attending?'

'Very. Pull out all the stops. My assistant will ring you with details of tonight's engagement.' He watched her closely. 'Why? Is that a problem?'

Rapidly she considered the clothes hanging in her enormous walk-in wardrobe. She had dressy clothes, including a black cocktail dress that she'd worn more times than she cared to remember. But there was formal and then there was formal. She didn't have the sort of outfits Rafe Benton would expect from his mistress. Definitely no ballgowns.

'My wardrobe doesn't currently run to glamorous.'

His instant look of disbelief turned into the hint of a smirk. 'So your luggage was full of sexy lingerie and nothing else?'

'No!' she snapped.

'You disappoint me, Antonia.'

For a moment the gleam in his eyes looked almost teasing. Then it faded.

'You sent your formal clothes home? That didn't show much foresight.'

There was no point in explaining that she didn't have formal clothes. Or a home.

'Well, you've got all day. You can go shopping and pick up something suitable.'

She shook her head. She had no money left for a spending spree—even if she had any longer term use for the sort of designer ballgowns he'd expect her to wear.

'What's the problem now? You've got the whole of London to choose from and a substantial chunk of my money in your account. Surely you can find something suitable?'

Except she didn't have his money. But she wasn't explaining the intimate details of her life to him. Pride was all she had left. Besides, he wouldn't be interested in that, just in her capacity to fill the role of mistress.

'You didn't tell me I'd be expected to buy a whole new wardrobe,' she said, her gaze sliding from his to the busy street as they travelled through the financial district.

Silence. A long silence.

'You really are a greedy piece of work, aren't you, sweetheart?'

She hated it when he called her that. Especially when he used that slow, mocking drawl.

'Haven't you screwed enough out of this deal already?'

'I'm merely pointing out that you didn't specify I'd be expected to outlay for a new wardrobe. Especially the sort of clothes you're talking about.'

He said nothing. Eventually, reluctantly, Antonia

gave in to his silent command, turning to meet his eyes. They flashed fire and ice, a potent combination that made her shrink back in her seat.

At last he spoke. 'I can see I should have drawn up a written agreement. It would have saved considerable time. And money.' Each word bit into her flesh. 'So I'm to understand you're unwilling to use your newfound wealth to clothe yourself?'

Antonia met his look, but said nothing.

'You know, I'm in half a mind to have you go naked.'

Her hiss of dismay was loud in the silence. He couldn't be serious. But, reading the sharp disdain in his expression, Antonia realised Rafe Benton might just follow through on that threat. Not in public, but in the privacy of his apartment. Her mouth dried at the very thought.

'Now I think of it, the idea is rather appealing.'

No! Surely he wouldn't.

'Perhaps to you,' she bit out, racking her brain for something to distract him from the idea. 'But if I come down with flu it would interfere with your plans.'

His gaze held hers so long her breathing grew shallow and her heartbeat raced as she waited for his response.

'We couldn't have that, could we? I don't want you flat on your back with illness.'

His searing look and the mocking edge to his

voice told her it wasn't the flat on her back bit he objected to. Her stomach cramped.

'All right, Antonia. I'll have my assistant set up a credit account for you to buy your clothes.' The tension was easing slightly from her shoulders when he continued. 'We'll stick to the letter of our bargain, sweetheart. Which means that you'd better deliver precisely what we've agreed. Understood?'

No mistaking the threat in those smooth tones.

Antonia swallowed convulsively. 'Understood.'

'Good. I want you looking spectacular tonight. Don't disappoint me.'

The car swung over to the side of the road and Antonia looked to see they'd parked in front of an imposing office block. This must be where Rafe's office was—

Her thoughts crashed to a halt when she felt his thigh against hers. His hand cupped her jaw and turned her to face him. He was crammed up against her in the corner of the car, pushing her back into the seat as he leaned close.

His eyes glittered as his gaze met hers, then roved her face, settling at last on her mouth. Heat burst through her at the intensity of that look. Heat and expectation. Convulsively she swallowed as unwanted awareness shivered through her.

His thumb swiped across her mouth, tugging her bottom lip down, her mouth open.

'Excellent. I'm glad we understand each other at last.' His breath was a warm puff of air on her lips.

Then his mouth was on hers, his tongue staking blatant claim. His kiss was thorough, deep, flagrantly erotic, even though he kept both hands splayed over her jaw and neck. He didn't paw her, or use his size to subdue her. Yet, to her shock, her body responded, heating with excitement at the sensations spearing through her. He took his time marking his possession. Darts of fire arrowed to erogenous zones she'd not known about as his tongue and lips worked magic.

Melting awareness spread through her, centering in her hollow aching core as he demonstrated a devastating sensual expertise.

His kiss was drugging, an invitation to pleasure unlike anything she'd known. Inevitably Antonia surrendered to the power of it, responding to the dance of his tongue against hers, the overpowering need to answer his caresses.

For long, glorious moments she felt the delicious excitement of pleasure given and shared.

Then he pulled away and she was left bereft, staring into eyes that sparkled with masculine satisfaction and a glint that might even be amusement. He looked completely unmoved and far too smug, while she battled to find her breath and her wits. A horn honked and she started, realising they'd been kissing in a busy street.

'It's a good thing the limo has tinted windows,' Rafe purred, allowing his hand to trail down her throat to her breast in a possessive caress that made her senses sing. And made her want to slam his hand away.

His lips curved into a devilish smile. 'I'm looking forward to tonight.'

CHAPTER SEVEN

SHE didn't disappoint.

That evening Rafe emerged from his suite, shrugging on his jacket, to find Antonia in the sitting room, absorbed in the vista of city lights.

From where he stood there was only one view worth looking at. His nerves pulled to jangling attention. Even wearing a long concealing coat, she was arresting. A red dress flared around her feet, and a glimpse of a stiletto heel caught his interest. He'd yet to see Antonia's legs, but he'd imagined them often enough: bare and silky smooth. A pair of sexy shoes made the picture perfect.

His groin tightened instantly on the thought.

She'd put her hair up again, less severely this time. It looked soft, seductive, as if a single tug would pull those tresses loose to tumble down her back.

Wearing her hair like that was a blatant invitation.

A moment later he'd bent his lips to the warm flesh at her nape, inhaling her exotic cinnamon scent. Was it a perfume or the natural fragrance of her skin? It had an instant impact on his libido. Or maybe it was the feel of her slim, feminine body as he drew her back against him.

She stiffened, then relaxed into his embrace. After the fire that had flashed in her eyes this morning Rafe had expected her to protest more. Perhaps his warning about delivering on her promises had worked.

Whatever. He was too busy nuzzling the side of her throat, sensing the tiny tremors running across her skin, to worry about her motivation. The feel of her so close, so tempting, threatened to divert him from his purpose. Delicious as she was, he couldn't afford to be sidetracked.

'Mink?' he murmured, as he stroked the fur. It was the perfect excuse to learn the shape of her supple body.

'Of course not.' She stiffened again, ramrod straight in his arms. 'It's *faux* fur.'

'You don't approve of wearing animal skins?' he whispered as he kissed behind her ear, not really giving a damn what she was wearing, but wanting to hear her voice again. It had a husky edge that turned him on.

She had other ideas. She tugged out of his arms, spinning round to face him. He had an impression of wide, glowing dark eyes, that gorgeous oval Madonna face, and perfect lips painted a glossy ruby-red.

The impact rocked him. She'd always looked sexy in that cool, classy way of hers. But now she looked *hot.* Red-hot. Those lips were full, sultry, luscious. A temptress's mouth.

Pity about the quelling schoolmarm look. But if she thought it would scare him off she was miles out.

'This is just as warm as fur. It looks as good and it's as soft. Why would I want mink?'

'For the same reason any woman wants to wear an exclusive label. For the prestige. To know that her man has paid a fortune so she can wear something obscenely expensive and flaunt her good luck.'

Her eyes narrowed and her head tilted assessingly.

'You really have a low opinion of women, don't you?'

He shook his head. 'Absolutely not. I've known some extraordinary women. But I'm experienced enough to know that there are plenty who see conspicuous consumption as a badge of honour—proof of their status.'

'Like me, I suppose?' She snapped out the words in bite-sized chunks, and Rafe sensed she'd like to sink those pearly whites into his flesh.

'If the shoe fits, sweetheart.' She was amazingly open about her greed. In his book that meant she had no right to pretend to false virtue. If there was one thing he abhorred it was a woman who pretended affection to get her grasping talons into a man's pocket.

Her nostrils flared disdainfully and she drew

herself up straighter. He waited for the inevitable riposte, but instead her features iced over. The vivid light of battle was quenched, replaced by smooth, impassive blankness.

His brows tugged together. He infinitely preferred her sassy to silent. There was a vibrancy about her when she argued, or kissed, that was much more appealing than her snow princess act.

'No argument? No backchat?' he baited.

She curved her lips in the tiniest of smiles. He could have sworn he heard ice crackling at the movement. He faced her haughty look. That was when he realised the sass hadn't disappeared. It was just hidden.

Antonia Malleson was one intriguing woman.

'I thought you specified that you required *compliance* in your mistress.' She paused. 'But, since you raise it, I'd prefer not to be called "sweetheart".'

'Of course…darling. I'm always willing to be *flexible*—especially when it comes to pleasing a woman.'

Something glinted in her eyes. Disapproval? Distaste? Or curiosity?

'You only have to ask and I'll do my best to satisfy you,' he promised.

'I thought that was *my* role. To satisfy *you*.' She tilted her chin higher, as if daring him to contradict her. 'Isn't that why you bought me?'

Dissatisfaction niggled at her description of their

arrangement. Strange, he'd never objected to plain speaking before, and it made a refreshing change from the usual female double-speak. Maybe it was because this was the first time he'd *bought* a lover. He was still acclimatising to the concept.

'Pleasure is a two-way street,' he responded. 'You don't think I'd demand satisfaction and not return the favour?'

Her eyes held his without blinking. He couldn't read a damned thing there. Meanwhile he felt the heat of sexual arousal roar into life, igniting his lower body. Just the mention of sex with her did that to him.

'I wouldn't presume to expect anything.' Her tone was clipped, but he spied the telltale pulse at her throat, beating frenetically. Beneath that façade of *sangfroid* she was as intrigued by the prospect of sex as he.

Rafe was tempted to taste that lush mouth. Yet they were late, and he had important business tonight. With the man he'd come to England to destroy. He contented himself with an almost chaste kiss at the corner of her mouth, then pulled back and drew her arm through his.

Strange how much he was looking forward to this evening in her company, and not just the impending prospect of sex. Nor did his anticipation centre solely on the idea of flaunting her in front of Stuart Dexter. Something about his clashes with Antonia Malleson made his blood pump faster. With something more than sexual stimulation.

One day he'd have to make time to figure out what it was.

Forty minutes later Rafe stared into the face of the man who was his father. He felt not one iota of connection, no qualms about activating his plan for revenge.

The memory of his mother's long drawn-out suffering kept his purpose firm. This man was despicable.

Satisfaction warmed him as he read Dexter's body language. An outer gloss of world weariness, a been-there-seen-it-all demeanour. But Rafe was astute enough to know it hid nervousness, even desperation. He smiled.

Dexter interpreted it as encouragement.

'Amazing coincidence, us being at the same ski resort.'

'Amazing,' Rafe agreed, watching Dexter adjust his bow tie. The man was anxious. Anxious enough to drop everything and run back to London the instant Rafe indicated he was ready to talk business. He was desperate for Rafe to bankroll his company's next move. It would be Rafe's pleasure to lend him a hand…straight to ruin.

'So, you're obviously giving this proposal your personal consideration. Excellent.' Dexter smiled.

The sort of toothy grin you'd expect from a used-car salesman.

'I always prefer to deal with the man in charge. It saves time,' he continued pompously. 'Forget the clutter of lawyers and accountants. Show me the man at the head of a business, and I'll tell you whether we can deal together.'

'You like to cut through the red tape?'

'Why fetter ourselves with unnecessary clutter?'

'To keep things legal and above board?' Rafe queried.

'Of course. Of course. Yet between like-minded men it's the gentlemen's agreement that counts.'

Rafe nodded, letting Dexter continue his spiel. Was this how he'd separated so many investors from their money? With talk of gentlemen's agreements?

Dexter wasn't precisely a crook—not that Rafe could prove—but he gave the financial regulators a run for their money. His business dealings pushed the legal limits.

But while Dexter had a flair for finance and a reputation for success, he didn't have the discipline to stay on top. For every successful move there were cases of unsound judgement too. In his wake small investors had lost everything, while he slithered out of the morass and started anew.

When you looked at it like that, Rafe had a civic duty to put an end to Dexter's wheeling and dealing. His private revenge would do an immense amount of public good.

It took a moment to realise the other man's patter had faltered, his attention on the other side of the room.

Rafe knew what Dexter had seen. Or rather whom. He stifled a smile at Dexter's absorbed reaction. Securing Antonia as his mistress had been a master stroke.

She'd excused herself as soon as they'd arrived at the Banqueting House in Whitehall. She'd murmured about freshening up, and Rafe had agreed to meet her inside.

Even through the crowd she was easy to spot. Her bright dress stood out like a beacon. His lips twitched. He'd specified that she did not fade into the background. There was no danger of that! Heads turned as she passed, gazes arrested, and Rafe felt a wholly male satisfaction at the knowledge that she was his. Or soon would be.

Then some of the suits parted and he caught a full-length glimpse of her. His heart hammered and his mouth dried. Heat burned along his skin as he took her in.

Hell!

Surely she'd been poured into that dress? He watched the way it hugged her, moving like liquid silk as she moved, covering and yet caressing every curve, every feminine dip and flare. How she managed to walk so serenely through the throng he didn't know. The dress followed the sleek contours of her waist, hips and thighs, only widening at the bottom, to flirt around her feet as she moved.

She was dynamite. Sex on a pair of teetering high heels. His blood pressure rose just at the sight of her.

Suddenly he wanted to forget about this evening's commitment and head straight back to the apartment.

Leaving Dexter gawping, he shouldered his way through the crowd that clustered about her. All male, he noticed.

Her eyes met his, and he could have sworn he saw uncertainty in her expression. But it must be a trick of the light. This was no hesitant damsel. A woman who could wear that dress with insouciance was sexually confident and supremely sure of herself. A siren, not a shrinking violet.

She'd been silent on the way here, as on their trip to London. He'd actually pondered whether he'd done the right thing, bringing her tonight. It wasn't long since she'd lost her father. Rafe had even wondered if his assessment of her had been too simplistic. Maybe she *was* grieving.

But no mourner dressed like that. It wasn't grief she felt as she played up to all the male attention. If she had anything else on her mind, it was only devising her next ploy to part him from his cash.

Rafe had to use force to push his way through the men crowding closest around her. He frowned. You'd think they'd never seen a woman before.

'Antonia.' His voice sounded unexpectedly rough.

'Rafe.' She looked up at him and curved her lips into the slightest of smiles. Its impact thundered through his chest. This was the first time her smile hadn't held sarcasm or superciliousness. The effect was hypnotic. Dimly he realised she was only delivering what he'd demanded. The appearance of intimacy. But that didn't lessen the effect.

He reached out and took her hand, drawing her near, staking his ownership.

Strange how the avid attention of every male in the place annoyed him. He always dated gorgeous women, so he was used to envy. This should be no different.

'Quite an entrance you've made,' he whispered. 'If this is your idea of *not fading into the background*, I'd love to see what you'd do if I asked for *eye-catching*.'

She shrugged one shoulder, and he watched the slinky material move with her body. It didn't matter that it covered her from neck to toe. This was gift wrapping any man would itch to rip away.

Rafe wanted to stroke the fabric, to feel her heat and her delicious curves through it. But he had a purpose in bringing her here: to show her off to Stuart Dexter. To show him that she was beyond his reach now.

His jaw hardened at the sudden, sickening memory of her and Dexter together at that resort nightclub.

Dexter's hands pawing at her, his body pressing into hers.

Had Dexter's obsession with her been due to the fact that he'd yet to get her into his bed?

Or had they been lovers? Had she displayed that sultry body for Rafe's father? An invisible vice squeezed the air from his lungs at the thought.

'Come on,' he urged in a voice of gravel. He put his arm round her. 'There are people I want you to meet.'

His hand touched flesh. Bare, warm, satin-smooth. Rafe stilled. His fingers splayed over the indentation of her spine, then slid lower to the dip of her waist. The only fabric he encountered was a narrow lacing, presumably keeping the dress from slipping straight off her.

She met his look steadily, her eyebrows raised just a fraction, as if in query.

What was she wearing? There was precious little to the front of the dress, despite the fact that it covered everything. He'd assumed at least it would have a back.

He lowered his voice. 'I'm wondering how much this dress cost if you thought I could only afford half of it.'

He surprised a smile out of her—a genuine one this time. It was glorious, intriguing, and far too short.

'Believe me, Rafe...' She paused on his name and his skin tingled at the sound of it on her tongue.

'You can afford it. You said you wanted glam, and this *is*.'

It was more than glam. It was sinfully sexy. Beyond provocative, it was downright blatant. He knew exactly what message it sent to every male in the vicinity. That was why he had to stifle the urge to bundle her back into her concealing coat.

Rafe frowned as he ushered Antonia into the penthouse. In the thick silence, he pondered what had gone wrong.

Showing off Antonia as his woman had worked like a charm. Dexter had all but salivated over her in his eagerness to get close. Nor had Rafe missed the glint of chagrin, of anger, in the other man's face as he watched them together.

Antonia had been superbly indifferent, cool and haughty, deigning to respond to Dexter only when absolutely required. That had made Dexter fume even more.

To Rafe's astonishment, she'd even made a show of nestling close to his side, cosying up, so he'd spent most of the evening with his arm wrapped round her. She'd been a distracting armful. His mind had kept wandering as he'd touched her bare back and tried to concentrate.

But, instead of triumphing at Dexter's frustration, Rafe had spent the evening unsettled and increasingly annoyed. Men had clustered around Antonia like dogs around a juicy steak. Those she hadn't seduced with her here-I-am-take-me outfit, she'd charmed. Rafe had spent the evening keeping the wolves at bay.

Not how he'd planned to spend his time.

Who'd have expected her to converse so knowledgeably with one of the National Gallery's most august patrons about the venue's remarkable ceiling? Who cared that it was the only such painting by Rubens still in its original location? Or that there'd been a *simply marvellous* recent exhibition of Dutch masterpieces?

Rafe had been stunned. He'd assumed her area of special expertise was designer labels.

'I don't know how you can stay up so late socialising and then put in a full day's work,' Antonia said, as he shut the apartment door behind them. 'Unless you have a late start tomorrow?' She knew she was babbling, but here, suddenly alone with him, she was aware only of his silent looming presence. And of the proximity of the bedrooms just down the hall. Tension held her rigid.

She'd spent the whole day trying not to think about this moment. She'd had two days' reprieve from his bed. She'd be a fool to expect any more.

'No late start. It will be a normal working day.'

She felt his eyes on her, grazing heat across her skin. Instead of meeting his look, she turned towards the kitchen. Maybe a cup of tea would soothe her nerves.

'Not so fast.'

Antonia stiffened at his harsh tone.

Not now. Please not now.

She was dizzy with fatigue. Grief and anxiety still kept her awake each night. Then there'd been tonight's shock. Her flesh crawled as she remembered being confronted with Stuart Dexter, Rafe's business associate.

She'd taken refuge in Rafe's presence, sidling closer to his protectively large body. She'd known Dexter wouldn't try anything while she was with Rafe, despite the thwarted fury she'd read in his expression. It had been weak of her, relying on the Australian's greater strength, but it had got her through the evening.

'I'm awfully tired.' And her head was beginning to throb. A stress headache.

'Nevertheless, we need to talk.'

Talk? Relief eased her taut shoulders.

He stalked round to stand before her, hands thrust in his trouser pockets, legs planted wide. There was a hint of dark shadow on his jaw that another woman might think enhanced his sexy appeal. She shoved aside the recollection of how his skin's intriguing scent had tickled her senses all evening.

Antonia watched Rafe's jaw harden, his blue eyes flash a warning signal. Just like when she'd walked into the reception tonight. Then she'd experienced a dangerous thrill, knowing she'd surprised him, punctured his self-assured certainty that he was in control of everything. But her delight in standing up to him had long since faded.

'That dress. I don't want to see you in it again.'

That caught her full attention. It was the last thing she'd expected to hear.

It had taken all her resolve to wear this dress. She'd known that if she didn't meet Rafe's demands head-on, with sheer bluff, she'd sink into self-pity. She couldn't afford that if she was to survive the next six months.

She'd made her bed—oh, how she hated that expression—and she had to lie in it. That didn't mean she'd let him browbeat her into submission. Her body might be his to possess, but she was determined he'd know she still had a mind and a will of her own.

She couldn't hide her new mistress status, so she'd decided to flaunt it, and show Rafe his temporary ownership meant nothing. She'd found much-needed strength tonight in the gesture of defiance. It had helped her keep her chin up despite the knowing looks and quizzical murmurs.

'You don't like it?' She lifted one eyebrow, her headache fading as combative energy sizzled.

'I expect you to draw a distinction between looking glamorous and looking…overly provocative.' There was an edge to his words that told her he wasn't happy.

Good. Nor was she. She shrugged off her long coat and draped it over a chair, feeling his eyes on her.

She shouldn't enjoy baiting him so much. It was

far too dangerous. But his glowering disapproval sparked an inexplicable recklessness in her. And surely that was better than sinking into despair.

'The most glamorous fashion designs *are* provocative.'

'I want you looking classy,' he bit out. 'Not like some cheap hooker.'

'Goodness.' Deliberately she widened her eyes. 'The prostitutes in Australia must be very well dressed. This is from a *very* exclusive boutique.' One of the few that sold quality fashion second-hand at knock-down prices.

Old habits died hard. It wasn't the first time she'd stretched her budget by snaffling a bargain there. But let Rafe think she'd spent a fortune on his credit card. That was what he'd expect.

'Don't play the innocent with me,' he growled. 'You know what I mean.'

'Frankly, I don't. You wanted me to look eye-catching, so I wore red.' She raised her hand and ticked off one finger. 'You wanted glamorous. This dress is designed on classic lines.' Another finger ticked off. 'You wanted something appropriate for tonight. This is a formal dress, and unique to boot.' Tick.

'What about the back of it?'

She tilted her head to one side consideringly. 'You're surely not telling me, as an experienced man of the world, that a little bit of bare skin is a problem?'

'More than a little.' He spoke through gritted teeth.

Antonia shrugged. 'You'd see more on any beach. And besides, it's just my back. No cleavage, no bare legs.'

With a single stride he closed the space between them. His azure gaze was so bright it should have scorched her, but after the emotional turmoil of the last few days she must be immune. Suddenly she was reckless, beyond fear.

'No arguments, Antonia. You won't win.' He glared down at her as if he'd like to shake her into submission. And still the unexpected surge of energy kept her from caring.

'No more backless dresses. Understood?'

'Yes,' she drawled, refusing to be cowed. 'Master…'

Somehow she wasn't at all surprised when he yanked her close and took her mouth in a punishing kiss.

CHAPTER EIGHT

THE sensation of slamming up against his raging heat, his powerful body, his simmering anger, obliterated Antonia's sassy insolence instantly.

How could she even *pretend* to be provocative when every nerve in her body was in shock at the sensations bombarding her?

She felt the clamp of his hands, his arms binding her close, his broad chest crowding her so she couldn't breathe. His tongue plunged into her mouth, possessing her intimately with the brazen confidence of ownership.

The contact lasted only a few moments then, abruptly, he released her. She rocked back on her heels, stunned by his withdrawal, dragging in deep, shocked breaths.

Heat flared in his stunning eyes and her heart plummeted. Her pulse throbbed a frantic beat.

Staring into those eyes, she knew with a sinking heart that it had come. *The moment of reckoning.*

* * *

Anger churned inside Rafe. He'd been patient, civilised, more than reasonable. She'd tested his goodwill to the limit. She'd even distracted him from his purpose. These last few days, his mind had wandered from his tricky negotiations and his plans for Stuart Dexter's ruin.

He'd promised to attend the reception tonight, especially as he'd known it would make Dexter sick with jealousy to see him with Antonia. Yet all evening he'd wanted nothing more than to be alone with her.

Satisfaction tinged his annoyance. Now they were—*completely* alone.

Wordlessly he reached for her hand. It was cool, like his mistress. The woman who'd milked him so expertly of his money. It was about time she gave something in return.

Her eyes met his, questioning. He swung her round and strode down the hall to her room, pulling her with him.

'Rafe?' She sounded breathless. He liked it.

Switching on a light, he drew her inside. Lamplight caught the fluid slide of slinky material over her breasts. Teasing little witch! This was going to be a real pleasure.

He placed her hand at his waist. Instantly tremors rayed out under his skin, shooting down his leg and into his groin. Her hand was slim, delicate, feminine. He couldn't wait to find out how it felt on his bare flesh.

'You had a pleasant time this evening?' he said, revelling in a moment's anticipation.

'I...yes. Thank you. Did you?' Her tone was thin, as if her mind were elsewhere. As if his conversation was of little interest. She fixed her gaze over his shoulder.

But he *was* significant. He'd paid for her delightful company—as she'd remember soon enough.

'It wasn't bad.' He slid his palm across her hand, where it rested on his jacket, enjoying the soft texture of her skin warming beneath his, the imprint of her hand on his body. 'But the night's not over yet.'

Looking into the velvet depths of her eyes, he was suddenly tired of this cat-and-mouse game. He knew what he wanted and he was going to get it. *Now.*

'So, Antonia.' His voice lowered to a deep murmur that drew her skin shivery tight. 'I do believe it's time to consummate our arrangement.'

His bright gaze drew her in, like a helpless moth to a flame. He had her now, and he revelled in the knowledge, in the sheer masculine greed for sexual satisfaction.

Antonia gulped down the clogging distress blocking her throat. She wasn't a helpless victim. She refused to be. The only way she could prevent herself from sinking into helpless despondency was to play the part she'd signed on for. Become his willing mistress and hope to salvage her autonomy by thinking of this purely as a mechanical, physical thing. By divorcing her emotions.

A wave of desolation roared through her.

No! She'd pick up the pieces later, when she was alone.

Antonia's breath snared as she watched him shrug out of his jacket and toss it over a chair. Then he reached for his midnight-blue bow tie. Seconds later it hung loose, a tantalising adornment to his strong, bronzed throat.

Deft fingers flicked open the first few shirt buttons, leaving her staring at a V of bare flesh.

Panic should set in now. Revulsion at what she was about to do.

But instead of horror Antonia discovered something else as Rafe lifted her hand to his chest. Shock reverberated through her at the raw explosion of need ricocheting inside her. What was happening to her?

Involuntarily her fingers splayed wide across the hard, cushioned muscles of his chest. As if she could absorb his masculine essence, the potent life force that emanated from him. It roused her dormant body to instant awareness and a welling sense of longing.

'Yes. Touch me, Antonia.' Rafe gathered her to him, his hands gliding down her back, dipping to follow the indentation of her spine. Then lower, to curve over her buttocks and squeeze. His body was all heat and hardness, his erection blatant against her.

Perversely, she felt no repugnance, no hesitation,

only a strange urgent hunger that spiralled tight within her.

How was it possible?

Rafe tilted his hips and a rush of moist heat pooled between her legs.

She wanted him—welcomed his brazen arousal!

Urgent sensations she'd never before known ran riot through her. Each nerve clamoured for more: of his touch, of his body, of his heat that warmed her as nothing ever had.

'Yes, like that,' he urged. Then his head blotted the lamplight and he took her mouth. Behind closed eyes Antonia was aware of him with every inch of her body. She drew his heady musk scent deep into her lungs, experienced the raw power of his sensuality as he melded her against him, kissed her till her head spun.

She told herself she responded because she had no choice. But it was a feeble lie. She wanted—

Strong hands on her shoulders pried her away from him. Glittering eyes the colour of paradise stared down at her as she fought to regulate her breathing. Her pulse raced, her body trembled with the force of unaccustomed desire. If he could do that to her with just a kiss…!

'Take your clothes off,' he said, pushing her back.

Antonia blinked, stunned by his abrupt tone, missing his embrace.

He sat down, and she realised they'd moved across to the bed without her realising. He spread his arms wide on the coverlet and leaned back, bracing himself on his hands.

'Strip for me,' he ordered.

Wordlessly she stared at him, searching for a trace of humour, a hint that he was kidding. She waited.

His mouth curled up at one side in a parody of a smile. His eyes wore a hooded expression of salacious intent, of impatience—like a petulant sultan, growing annoyed with a recalcitrant concubine.

He was serious. One dark brow rose in mocking interrogation. It was the look she'd dubbed his fallen angel expression. Haughty, challenging, utterly superior.

That's what you get for taunting a man like Rafe Benton. He'd probably stored up the memory of each time she hadn't toed the line, hadn't jumped instantly to his bidding. Now he intended to make her pay.

First he'd humiliate her. Then he'd sate himself in her body. Horrible crawling embarrassment slithered across her skin, leaving it tight and cold. She wanted to wrap her arms about herself and hide from that despoiler's gaze. But she couldn't escape.

He was opening his mouth, no doubt to reiterate the order, when, with a sudden desperate energy, she reached for the shoulders of her dress, wrenching them down her arms with total disregard for the delicate fabric. She shrugged out of both sleeves till the dress hung from her waist.

The air was cold, raising gooseflesh on her skin. She felt her nipples tug into tight peaks. Whether from the chill, or the fact that he surveyed her with proprietary intensity she didn't know. He must be aware of her reaction. It would be visible even beneath the red bra that had been designed to match the delicate laces at the back of the dress.

Antonia couldn't watch him as she lowered the side zipper then pushed the fabric down over her hips. She let her eyes glaze to an unfocused blur. It was easy with moisture pricking them.

She had to shimmy out of the clinging dress, but eventually managed to push it down till it slid to pool around her feet. Ice-hot shame seared her.

Gingerly she stepped to one side and bent to undo the tiny straps on her shoes.

'No! Leave them.' His voice seemed hoarse, but Antonia knew it was just that she couldn't hear properly over the rushing sound in her ears.

She fixed her eyes on the sheer curtains tied beside the bed as she lifted her hand to the front clasp of her bra. Her fingers shook so much she couldn't undo it.

She bit the inside of her cheek as she tried to steady herself. No matter how he tried to humiliate her, she refused to let Rafe Benton know how well he'd succeeded. She couldn't let him guess how much this cost her.

Mortification filled her as she realised how unthinkingly she might have given herself if only he'd continued kissing her. She'd been putty in his hands.

And he'd known it. But obviously that hadn't been enough for his jaded tastes. He'd needed to torment her too.

'Come here,' he ordered. 'There are some things a man prefers to do himself.'

Every muscle froze to rigidity. Bad enough to provide the floor show. But the idea of his hands on her body…

Her stomach cramped in a spasm of pure dismay. She ignored it and stepped close, till she stood within the V of his spread legs. The heat of his body curled around her, but it couldn't warm her. She was chilled to the marrow.

Lifting her chin, she kept her eyes fixed on the swathe of bed curtains. Maybe if she didn't look she could pretend this wasn't real.

But the feel of his long fingers deftly flicking open her bra was all too real. Antonia sucked in a breath as he slid the straps off her shoulders and it fell away.

Silence.

She squeezed her thighs tight together, trying to stop the trembling in her legs. Cool air caressed her breasts, and despite her best intentions she drew a deep shuddery breath that pushed her nipples forward towards him as he sat so still and silent.

What next? Was she supposed to discard her knickers too? Heaven help her, she had no knowledge to draw on here.

'You really are beautiful, aren't you?' he whispered roughly. 'But obviously you know that.'

It sounded like an accusation. Antonia frowned. What did he want her to say?

Then all thought suspended as his hands closed on her breasts, cupping them, moulding, massaging. Her breath was a hiss of desperation as unfamiliar sensations shot through her.

'You like that?' No mistaking the satisfaction in his gravel-deep tone.

But Antonia didn't answer. She was too busy stiffening herself against the strange laxness that had attacked her muscles. She wasn't going to fall in a heap at his feet, no matter how insidiously wonderful the feelings he evoked.

His thumb and forefinger tightened, tweaking her right nipple, and a jolt of fiery heat shot straight through her.

'Ah, you're very sensitive.'

She hated his smug tone almost as much as she hated her body's betrayal. How could she respond when he was so callous in his treatment of her?

She'd always believed that she'd only respond physically to a man if she were in love with him. Or believed herself to be, as she had with Peter. How appallingly little she knew about herself.

'So I think you'll like this.'

Antonia jumped as his mouth closed on her nipple.

'Steady,' he murmured, and she felt his lips on her

sensitive skin. One strong arm wrapped around her back to hold her close against him. His other hand was warm and surprisingly gentle, cupping her breast as he sucked.

Antonia's knees threatened to buckle at the scorching comet of heat and need that burned its way across her consciousness. Her eyes fluttered shut and she swayed towards him, pressing into him, revelling in the ecstasy of his mouth working her flesh. It felt... unbelievable.

Not so unbelievable as the unmistakable flood of moist arousal at her core. Again she tensed her legs, this time trying to counter the warm gush. She didn't want to be turned on. She *shouldn't* be. And yet undeniably her body was responding to his ministrations. He ran his tongue over the underside of her breast and all her muscles clenched.

'Open your eyes,' he demanded.

She opened them to slits against the light.

'Now look at me.'

Slowly, reluctantly, Antonia tilted her head down. Dark hair, blazing blue eyes, that long angular nose and... She reached out and grabbed his shoulders, needing to anchor herself. She watched his teeth nip at one rosy peak then move to the other. He licked her breast, from bottom to top, his eyes never leaving hers. Her fingers tightened like claws on the muscles of his shoulders as darts of pure desire shot with lightning force through her.

From under straight black brows his knowing eyes surveyed her, watching the effect of his caresses. There was nothing she could do. She couldn't dissemble. Not when she was melting at every deliberate touch, each gentle bite. He drew her nipple into his mouth and sucked hard, and she felt it straight through her belly, between her legs, in every erogenous zone in her body.

A low moan sounded in her ears and she realised it must be her. Yet she could barely care when he worked such magic on her.

Finally he raised his head, still watching her. Her breasts throbbed and it was all she could do not to thrust them forward, wordlessly demanding more.

'Now it's your turn,' he said. 'Undress me.'

The pulse drumming between her legs was almost strong enough to drown out her silent cry of denial.

But where could she go? Rafe would only haul her back. And the shaming truth was that, despite the humiliation of being ordered to please him, Antonia was excited by the experience. Secretly thrilled by the sweet torment of his mouth and hands on her breasts. Desperately eager for more, if more meant an ease to the compulsive urge for intimacy.

Her hands shook as she removed his cufflinks, but she got them out and dropped them into his waiting palm. He reached out and put them on her bedside table, along with something he drew from his pocket. Square foil packets. Several of them.

Her eyes rounded. Surely they wouldn't need so many?

'I like to be prepared,' Rafe said as he surged to his feet before her. This close his spicy musk scent tickled her nostrils. The sharp tang of it was different, more pronounced than before.

He lifted her hands to his half-open shirt. Now her movements were less clumsy. Maybe because with each button she revealed more of his dark bronze chest and torso.

Her mouth dried as she took in the masculine perfection slowly being revealed. She tugged his shirt out and spread it wide. A fuzz of dark hair crossed his pectorals. In the lamplight its shadow highlighted the pronounced definition of his muscles.

She'd known he was strong, but somehow he seemed bigger, more solid, without the layers of his suit and dress shirt. He was completely, blatantly masculine.

Antonia pushed the fine cotton from his shoulders and let it fall, aware of him with each straining nerve. She trembled, caught within his potent physical aura, her heartbeat erratic. If Rafe Benton hadn't been a corporate high-flier he'd have made a fortune as a male model. Her gaze trailed down his body and every inch was perfection.

'There's more,' he urged, in a dark, teasing voice.

Antonia blinked, jerked out of her abstraction. Still she refused to look him in the eye. She knew her limits.

Instead she knelt before him to undo his shoelaces. He'd enjoy that, no doubt, the sight of her obeisance. Desperately she tried to ignore his looming presence, but it was impossible. She felt too vulnerable.

Too soon his shoes and socks were discarded and she straightened, wobbling only slightly on the high heels. For a heartbeat she hesitated, steeling herself, then made herself reach for his belt. Her knuckles brushed his abdomen and the smooth skin that was pure invitation. It was like touching electricity—shock waves roared through her. For a moment her senses swam, then she noticed his reflexive move-ment—the drawing in of muscle, the tightening of skin. She paused, wondering.

Slowly she undid the buckle and loosened Rafe's belt. Then she reached for the fastening of his trou-sers, slipping her fingers inside, against the hot satin of his skin. Again that instant reaction. This time she could almost swear she heard a swift intake of breath.

The realisation buoyed her. Not so one-sided, then, despite Rafe's arrogance. Her hand was almost steady as she tugged the zip down, then pushed his trousers to the floor.

'And the rest,' he urged, his voice a low whisper.

Tentatively Antonia reached out and tugged his boxers down. There was a moment of delay as the fabric caught on his erection, but he helped her, freeing himself from the shorts and thrusting them impatiently out of the way.

Antonia tried not to stare, but it was impossible. Rafe Benton was beautiful all over. And the sight of his arousal, rampant and ready for *her*, was shamingly exciting.

Hurriedly she shifted her gaze, to find him tearing open one of the foil packets.

Her eyes darted to his face, taking in the stark lines of concentration there, the taut control. For all his measured movements, Rafe looked like a man on the edge.

'Here.' He pressed the condom into her hand and sat down on the bed.

'You want me to…?'

'Why not?' His smile was frayed. 'Practice makes perfect, and I'm sure you've had plenty of practice.'

Antonia gritted her teeth at the calculated insult. 'You may be surprised to discover that I've never…' She paused and swallowed. 'Never done this before.'

'What? Never fitted a condom?' His tone was incredulous. Then his eyes narrowed and he sat forward a little. 'Or are you trying to tell me you're a virgin?'

Flaming heat washed Antonia's face as she shook her head. 'No. Not that.' Though in truth she was only barely experienced.

'Good. I wouldn't like to think you'd added lying to your other accomplishments.' He leaned back and fixed her with a gimlet eye.

The self-satisfied, smirking—

'I'm ready when you are,' he taunted.

That much was obvious, she thought sourly. More than ready. So ready that she was nervous, wondering about the mechanics of this. She was tall, but he was so well endowed. Was that squiggle of tension in her stomach fear or excitement? She blanked her mind, trying not to think about it. Trying not to think about anything.

'Come on, Antonia. You do it this time and I'll do it next.' He smiled a wide, white taunting grin. 'I'm an equal opportunities lover.'

That stiffened her spine, Rafe saw. Not that it needed straightening. She was the perfect picture of haughty disdain. Even standing there in nothing but lace panties and the sexiest shoes he'd ever seen, she had the bearing of a queen. He watched her perfect high breasts sway as she knelt and his breath stopped deep in his lungs.

If he didn't have her soon, he'd explode. The combination of her cool touch-me-not air and the incredible sensuality of her response to his lightest caress had him groping for control. He'd had to pull back, establish some mental distance, so he didn't do something stupid like take her instantly, with no preliminaries and no precautions.

Antonia Malleson was the hottest woman he'd ever met. The sound of her husky voice moaning as he sucked at her breast had shorted something in his brain, welding shut the door on what was left of his self-possession.

He couldn't remember ever wanting a woman with quite this level of desperation.

Her slim fingers touched him and thought fled. He held his breath as tentatively, softly, her fingers fluttered over him. She fumbled with the condom, paused and tried again.

He wasn't breathing. His hands were clamped into the bedding and his body was tight as a high wire. Why hadn't he listened when she'd said she'd never done this before? She was killing him by degrees. It was sheer erotic torment having her touch him. Damn his need to score points with his taunting.

Afterwards Antonia couldn't recall exactly what happened next. It was a blur of rapid movement, of shockingly intimate, wonderful sensation. Within seconds, it seemed, Rafe had finished the job she'd barely begun, stripped away her shoes and her underwear, and she was caught in that mesmerising electric gaze.

She felt it flare again—the same heat that had pulsed between them when they'd met. A scorching force that rocked her to her core. She tried to hang on to her anger but her focus was shifting.

'No more games,' he growled. Then his arms were

around her and he pulled her onto the bed, his body warming hers, his hands creating fire with each slow swipe.

He took her face in his palms and kissed her. Not in a show of strength or domination this time but, it dawned on her, in mutual delight.

Her fear and even her fury fled as he coaxed, cajoled, tempted her into responding. She didn't recall giving up the fight to stay distant, whole, separate. For Rafe set about seducing her with expert caresses, whispered words of encouragement, and a look in his eyes that no woman could resist. That expression—intense pleasure, sultry invitation and something else that looked remarkably like tenderness—bypassed the last of her weak defences.

His hands were those of a lover: sure, gentle and knowing. He palmed her inner thigh, up one leg and down the other, slowing each time to touch her just…*there*, where her need burned brightest. He lingered, stroked, his caresses languorous, then purposeful. And through it all his eyes held hers captive.

Soon her body was alight with a blaze of desire. She welcomed him as he braced himself above her. There was no thought now of pride or honour or shame as she slipped her hands round his back, sliding them across his slick, hot skin. There was just this moment.

He paused, his chest heaving above her, the coarse

hair on his legs tickling her thighs. His warmth, his musky scent, his power encompassed her.

'Ready?' he surprised her by asking.

It didn't occur to her to say no. For this was what she wanted. Whether it was right or wrong, she craved this intimacy now with every particle of her being.

Wordlessly she nodded, and an instant later the world turned over, rocked off its axis by the sensation of his possession, their oneness. She had a moment only to absorb that stunning new reality and then it started, a trembling rush of heat that forged out through her body, tightening each muscle and sinew, shocking her with its intensity.

Antonia clutched at him wordlessly and he responded with another slow, deep thrust right to her core that unleashed the floodtide of exquisite sensation. Her eyes fluttered shut as her body found ecstasy. And through it she carried the image of his sky-blue eyes, heard his husky voice urging her on and on.

Then, just as she reached an impossible peak of pleasure, that perfect rocking movement faltered and he climaxed too. His body shook with the force of it, his guttural cry reverberated in her ears and she felt him pulse within her.

Antonia pulled him close, wrapping her arms tight round him as she sank into the bed, blanketed by his solid weight. Against all logic, she experienced a sense of rightness. It should be impossible. Yet what they'd shared was remarkable, mind-numbing. In the aftermath of bliss she didn't have the energy to question it.

After a few moments he moved, rolling onto his back, keeping her clamped to him as if he couldn't bear the thought of breaking that embrace any more than she could.

She felt safe in Rafe's arms, as if the grief and pain of the everyday world had been magically banished. Their hearts beat together, their urgent breaths in sync.

She tried to tell herself this was just sex. Better sex than she'd had with Peter. Better sex than she'd dreamed possible. Yet thinking it and believing it were two different matters.

An inner voice told her that it had just changed her life. Antonia closed her ears to it. That wasn't hard to do as Rafe lifted her chin with long fingers that shook just enough for her to notice. They stared at each other, and Antonia realised his eyes were glazed with the same shock that filled her. The same wonder. No trace now of the cocky autocrat who'd ordered her acquiescence to his whims.

'Antonia.' Even his voice sounded different—a raw, husky whisper.

Then he was kissing her, slowly, gently, as if she was the most precious thing in his world. She gave herself up willingly, reciprocating with caresses of her own.

* * *

The lamp was still on when she woke out of a haze of comfort, her body weighted with pleasure. Something had changed. The intense heat that had cradled her was missing.

Blearily she narrowed her eyes against the light, glancing at the bedside table with its litter of torn wrappers. It looked as if they had used them all.

A tiny thrill spiralled through her belly at the memory of how well loved she'd been. Of how perfect Rafe had made it for her, responding to needs she hadn't been aware she possessed.

She reached out a hand to him, realising she couldn't feel him against her. Abruptly she turned her head, hearing movement. She frowned as an invisible weight pushed down on her chest. Her breath seized under the pressure.

Rafe stood at the foot of the bed, his clothes a tumbled bundle in his naked arms. He looked gorgeously male, the lamplight gilding each powerful curve and plane of his body and glinting off the dark sheen of his rumpled hair. His surprisingly soft hair, through which she'd tunnelled her hands as they'd made love time after time.

Something like tenderness welled inside her.

Then his eyes met hers, and her pulse pounded loud in her head. He looked *different*. Gone was the intimacy, the shared pleasure of the past few hours. Instead his gaze was sharp, like honed steel.

'What are you doing?' Her voice was a ragged whisper as she spoke over rising foreboding.

'Collecting my clothes.' His forehead puckered, as if he was surprised at her question.

'Why?'

'I don't expect you to do my laundry, Antonia. I'm sure such domesticity wouldn't suit you.' His tone was cool, collected, matter-of-fact. Totally unlike the man who'd just shared her bed and what she'd thought in her innocence had been the most profound mysteries a man and a woman could experience together.

Her heart dipped. 'Why not?' Already she knew she wouldn't like the answer.

She was right.

'Because your talents obviously lie in other directions.' His gaze roved from her hair, loose around her shoulders, down the rumpled coverlet, to encompass the whole of the vast four-poster bed. His mouth curved up in a slow, satisfied smile that iced her veins.

'Sleep well.' He turned towards the door.

'Where are you going?' She couldn't keep the sharp edge from her voice.

Rafe paused and looked over his shoulder, his expression closed. 'I told you when we arrived, Antonia. I sleep alone. I'll see you tomorrow.'

The light clicked off and darkness enfolded her.

She'd just been dismissed. Used by the man who'd paid for her services, put firmly in her place, then set aside.

It was as if he'd slapped her across the face.

Reality crashed in, negating the joy they'd shared, the unexpected sense of peace she'd discovered in their intimacy. He'd smashed her fragile fantasy, reminding her this was a business transaction. *A sordid arrangement. Not a new beginning.*

Pain welled in all the places his touch had thawed.

She felt like a prostitute.

CHAPTER NINE

ANTONIA stared out of her bedroom window, her mind straying inevitably to Rafe. And how she'd morphed in his arms into a woman she didn't know.

Heat flooded her as she recalled their encounters. Her skin drew tight and tingling at the images shifting in her brain. Images of them entwined together, of the desire blazing in his eyes as he undressed her, of the eager way she'd matched his demands with a ravenous hunger of her own.

It had been a revelation. Despite her pride, her anger, her confusion, she could never resist him. Each time he drew her close her resistance crumbled and she grew willing, even wanton, in his arms.

There must be a sensible explanation. Maybe sex with Rafe was a physical outlet for the turmoil of raw emotions she'd clamped a lid on for so long. Heaven help her if her response had anything to do with genuine attraction.

Attraction? To the man who'd purchased her to warm his bed? She told herself that was impossible.

She frowned. Each night she played the part of devoted mistress, accompanying him to some society event and then later spending hours satisfying his more personal needs. He was a demanding lover, and a generous one. To her shame she found herself eagerly anticipating their lovemaking. It would be too easy to allow her own physical satisfaction to blind her to the fact that this was a business arrangement. He still left her to sleep alone. Never bothered to check if she was awake before leaving early for the office. It was his PA who called each day with details of that night's outing.

No, this was a thoroughly cold-blooded deal. She fitted a convenient niche in life. That was all.

A numbing fog enclosed her as she watched rain spatter the windows. Grief was still a yawning dark void inside. She was trapped in a role that outraged every sensibility, and there was no escape.

The wintry weather matched her mood: dull and listless. Even the solace of tears eluded her. She was closed up—her emotions, even her grief, locked away.

The only time she felt a spark of heat and life was when Rafe baited her into indignation or anger.

Or when he made love to her.

'Antonia. Are you ready?' Rafe's voice pulled her out of her reverie.

Hurriedly she scooped up her jacket, her beaded evening purse and opened the door, ignoring a skittering sensation that might be excitement. No, it was simply that she didn't want him entering her room.

'Ready,' she said, not quite meeting his eyes. He looked superb in evening dress. The contrast between the suave suit and his rugged handsomeness inevitably sent a twinge of awareness scooting through her.

Slowly he surveyed her and she held her breath, hating the way excitement pumped her blood faster.

'You look fantastic.' He took in her sleeveless top and trousers in slinky black threaded with gold.

His eyebrows rose as he saw her sandals: pure mistress material, with gossamer straps of rhinestones and four-inch spiked heels. One look had told her they were perfect for the role she was playing.

'And...' his lips tilted up in wry appreciation '...you have the sexiest feet.' His voice was a rich, low rumble that caressed her skin.

Astonishment froze her. She recognised with dismay the skirl of excitement his words evoked. She tensed.

'I'm glad you like glitter. I've brought you something I think you'll enjoy.' He stepped into the room, proffering a velvet case.

A gift? A second look confirmed her initial impression. There was no mistaking the jeweller's box. The zing of secret pleasure she'd felt at his arrival disintegrated.

'Aren't you going to open it?' He sounded more impatient than amused now.

Reluctantly she took the case and lifted the lid. Inside was a brilliant rope of stunning yellow diamonds. A long strand shaped as a pendant and a matching bracelet.

'You hired them?' she asked dully.

'No.' Even without looking up she could hear the frown in his voice. 'I bought them for you to wear tonight.'

'Thank you,' she said woodenly.

He wanted to flaunt his mistress and his wealth for all to see. He'd sell the pieces when she was gone. After all, she was expendable.

This reminder of their commercial arrangement hit her like a body-blow to the stomach. Antonia felt the last tattered shreds of her self-respect rip away as his big square hand dipped into the box and lifted the necklace. Her muscles cramped and her fingers tightened like claws on the plush velvet of the jewel case.

'You haven't worn any jewellery since we came to London.' No missing the question in his tone.

'No,' she said, her eyes fixed on this symbol of her degradation. 'It's not really my style,' she lied.

'Now, that surprises me.'

She darted her head up and found his gaze raking her, as if he could strip her bare of secrets. She shivered at the intensity of that look, feeling far too vulnerable.

'Your complexion is perfect for gold,' he said, with all the conviction of a man who'd no doubt adorned his previous mistresses with baubles and pricey trinkets. 'Like that pendant you wore in Switzerland. Opal, wasn't it?'

'Yes,' she said quickly and ducked her head, pretending interest in the diamonds. Why did he have to remember that? It had been her mother's favourite piece and Antonia had sold it with the rest of her jewellery. That had been her first act when she'd had a day alone in London.

A familiar ache began deep inside her—a burgeoning pain she battled to repress. All she had now of her mother was memories. She really was utterly alone.

'Here, let me,' he murmured. Deftly he clasped the bracelet around her wrist, then moved behind her to lower the pendant onto her bare neck. The icy metal burned her flesh like a brand. A brand of his possession.

His hands moved from her nape to her shoulders and he turned her to face the full-length mirror on the other side of the room. She concentrated on the sparkling necklace rather than the image of his tall body framing hers.

'Nothing to say, Antonia?' No mistaking his impatience.

'It's very beautiful,' she said, knowing it was the truth, but sickened at the realisation he'd bought her as easily as he had the jewellery.

What had she become?

Rafe looked at the reflection of her set face and wondered what in hell was wrong with her.

'Most women would be excited about a gift like that,' he prompted, annoyed that he'd let her get to him again.

'I'm sure you're right. It must have cost a lot of money.' She said it as calmly as if she didn't give a damn for the price—which he knew to be a lie. The thought infuriated him.

'Most women would show their thanks in a tangible way.' A kiss, even a smile would be a start.

He was tired of the way she clammed up, as if an impenetrable barrier cut her off from him. They only communicated when she let down her guard because he'd taunted her into a dispute. Then he'd see the vibrant woman behind the blank façade.

Or when they made love. Then it was as if she were another woman. Real and passionate and just as needy as he. Then the desire between them was so strong, so compelling, he had a hard time matching her to the aloof beauty who kept him at arm's length.

'I'm sorry. I've disappointed you.' He watched her reflection form the words. Her lips seemed curiously stiff.

She turned round to face him and he looked down into guarded dark eyes. Not even a flicker of satisfaction there. She must be the most cold-blooded woman he'd ever met. Yet a disturbing niggle in his gut told him she wasn't that straightforward.

Slowly Antonia lifted her arms. He caught the spangle of gems on one wrist as she looped her hands behind his head. Her fingers cupped his neck and his breathing quickened.

'How would you like me to thank you?' Her voice had that husky quality he loved. The throaty roughness that signalled her arousal. Only this time instinct told him it was some other emotion he heard in her voice.

Her lips touched his. Pliant, warm, enticing. Instantly, inevitably, heat roared through him.

'With a kiss?' The movement of her lips against his was an erotic invitation, and the feel of her leaning close sent his pulse thundering.

'Or something more?' She pulled back a fraction, letting cool air slide between them. He saw her tilt her head to look at her watch. 'We're due there in forty minutes. I don't know how important this reception is tonight.' Her eyes met his unblinkingly. 'Do you want to be on time?'

Rafe frowned at the sudden twist of discomfort in his stomach. It was the way she spoke, so cold-bloodedly, as if it made no difference to her whether they left now or whether he tumbled her back onto the bed.

He knew that wasn't true. He knew for a fact she was *always* satisfied with his loving. He made sure of it. She was as interested in their sex-life as he was, damn it!

He had no explanation for the crawling heat that spread under his skin. She couldn't have reinforced more clearly that he'd purchased her for his pleasure. To his chagrin, he discovered he wanted more. He wanted her willing and wanting. An equal partner, not a bought one.

He reached round and took her hands in his, dragging them from his shoulders and holding them before him. The gems of her new bracelet were hard and cold against his palm.

'No! You've done enough.' His tone was rough and her eyes widened.

Which was the real Antonia? The fiery seductress or the cold-as-frost woman calmly offering herself in recompense for the thousands of pounds worth of diamonds on her wrist?

He'd seen the golden fire in the stones and instantly thought of the way her eyes blazed when they made love. The purchase had been pure impulse. One he now regretted.

'Come on,' he grated. 'It's time we left.'

Two hours later Rafe looked down at the gorgeous woman beside him, baffled. Gone was the reserve that for one crazy moment he'd thought might be pain. Her mood had swung to one of hectic gaiety. She chatted animatedly, drawing men to her side effortlessly with her wit and her smiles.

Never before had he felt so wrong-footed. When he asserted his presence, made her acknowledge him, she devoted her attention to him with generous smiles, a hand on his sleeve, sparkling glances from lustrous eyes.

Yet her apparent intimacy felt unsatisfying. False. As if she were a consummate actress playing a game.

Annoyance twisted his mouth to a grim line. He'd counted on her acknowledging the powerful attraction between them by now. But she pretended it didn't exist.

'Let's dance,' he murmured in her ear, simultaneously drawing her aside.

'Dance?' She faltered to a stop.

'Yes. It'll give your admirers a chance to wipe the drool off their faces.'

Her brows arched. 'You're exaggerating.'

'I never exaggerate.' He swept a look down as he led her to the dance floor. He should have paid more attention to what she was wearing earlier, but he'd been preoccupied with her puzzling lack of response to the diamonds. It hadn't been until they'd arrived at the business awards ceremony that he'd seen the way her trousers swung as she walked, parting in long side-slits to reveal the perfection of her legs. She was barely decent.

If it weren't for the fact that he was giving a speech soon he'd take her straight home. But at least in a slow dance her outfit wouldn't draw too many eyes.

Rafe pulled her close, loving the feel of her soft body against his.

'I had an interesting conversation with my PA today.'

'You did?'

'Yes. There was some confusion with a couple of credit accounts, and she checked the expenditure on the one you've been using.'

Antonia raised her head at that, stiffening in his embrace. 'You've been checking up on me, you mean!'

He ignored that. Why the hell would he check up on a card he'd made available for her use?

'She said there'd been very little spent, despite the glamorous outfits you've been wearing.' His hand slid over the silky fabric at her back. She felt so good.

'And?'

'Why are you being so frugal with my money?' In the dimmed lighting it was hard to read her expression, but she was avoiding his eyes.

'I hadn't realised it was compulsory for me to be extravagant.' Her response was flippant.

He pulled her close, so she was flush against him. After a moment's resistance he felt her relax. His lips curved up in satisfaction.

'There's no need to get on your high horse. I'm not annoyed, just curious.'

She shrugged. 'Why spend a fortune on clothes I'm not going to keep?'

'Of course you'll keep them. They're yours.' Anger roughened his voice. Was she implying he'd take them from her when they parted?

She shook her head. 'In case I want to hook myself another wealthy man? No, thanks.'

Satisfaction jabbed him at the knowledge she wouldn't wear any of her sexy outfits for anyone else. Until he realised she'd probably demand any future lover bought her a complete new wardrobe. The very idea of Antonia with another man sent tension spiralling through him. His hands tightened on her and she looked up at him. Those dark eyes of hers were mesmerising, almost enough to distract him.

'How are you keeping the bills so low, Antonia? You might as well tell me. I'll find out eventually.'

Her chin jerked up as if he'd aimed a body-blow. Had he hit a nerve?

She turned her head and stared past his shoulder, as if the milling crowd held her interest.

'I bought them from a few places I know. They deal in second-hand fashion.'

Rafe couldn't believe his ears. He'd summed her up as too proud, too haughty, ever to stoop to wearing someone else's garments.

'You can pick your jaw up now,' she said tartly. 'It's not that unusual, you know. Lots of people do it.'

But he'd never imagined her to be one of them. 'I know.' Hell, he'd done it himself years ago. 'But why take the cheap option when you have access to my money?'

Was there ever a more puzzling woman?

'Habit, I suppose.' Her voice was so low he had to lean close to hear her.

'You've done this before?'

'It's nothing to be ashamed of!' She paused, as if waiting for him to change the subject. But he was intrigued.

'Go on.' He could feel her body stiffening again. But he'd question her all night if he had to.

'Money has always been tight. All right?' She glared at him, her mouth a flat line. 'My father never learned to economise, and the places we lived…well, there was rarely a cheap option.' She drew in a deep breath. 'Now, can we leave this?'

'Of course. On one condition. From now on you buy new. Understood?' No woman of his was going to wear hand-me-downs. He'd worked too long and hard to escape all that.

For a charged moment she held his gaze. Then abruptly she nodded. Strange how her capitulation felt like a victory. This information merely confirmed what he knew about her constant need for money. She moved in circles where wealth was taken for granted, but she had trouble keeping up appearances. No wonder she was on the make.

Yet there was something else here too. Something he couldn't quite put his finger on. If she was so greedy, why hadn't she taken advantage of his money and spent lavishly on herself?

He shook his head and pulled her to him, revelling in the feel of her delicious curves moving against him.

Would he ever understand this woman?

Antonia gave herself up to the heady pleasure of Rafe's embrace. The rhythmic swaying movement seemed so intimate. When he held her like this she felt absurdly safe and content. Almost…cherished.

The idea was ridiculous. But every so often, like now, she sensed there was another side to him. Apart from the demanding tycoon and the expert lover.

Why had he insisted on her buying new clothes for herself? Was it pride—he didn't want his mistress in second best? Or was it generosity?

He'd been generous in giving her the diamonds too. And she was pretty sure now that he had no idea how insulting she'd found the gift. He'd looked so stunned at her reaction. Almost hurt.

Hah! As if that were possible. Her being able to hurt the mighty Rafe Benton.

Yet there were other things that made her wonder about him. His unfailing politeness to staff, from doormen to waitresses. He treated them with the same courtesy he bestowed on the wealthy guests at functions like tonight's. His easy camaraderie with his chauffeur, the back and forth discussion on anything from football scores to politics and the achievements of young grandchildren.

In her experience, most mega-wealthy people preferred to forget that the people who drove them, or served them in some other way, were real people with lives of their own.

'That woman tonight,' she said suddenly, remembering the gorgeously dressed older woman. 'Barbara Havers.'

'Yes? What about her?' His voice came from just above her, muffled in her hair. She shut her eyes, enjoying the illusion of warmth and intimacy it engendered. She'd never enjoyed dancing with any man the way she did with Rafe.

'Is she an old friend?'

'I never met her before tonight. Why?'

'You got on so well, I wondered.' She paused, choosing her words carefully. 'Some people find it difficult or embarrassing at first, having a conversation with someone in a wheelchair.' She remembered the last stages of her mother's illness, when strangers would instinctively turn away from the frail seated figure.

'More fool them. It's the person, not the chair, you speak to.' There was something in his voice that made her raise her head.

His face looked curiously set, his jaw hard.

'My mother was in a wheelchair for years,' he said at last. 'So I know exactly what you mean.'

Was? Past tense? Had she recovered, or was she…? Antonia didn't have the nerve to pry.

'You spent a lot of time with her?'

'I was her primary carer for years.' His mouth thinned to a flat line and he stepped back as the music ended. Cool air rushed between them. Antonia felt curiously bereft.

The lights were turned up and she read grimness in his eyes. Bad memories, then. Something squeezed tight inside her at the sight of his pain; fellow feeling, perhaps. She too had personal experience of caring for an ailing parent, and of loss.

Instinctively she reached out and put her hand on his arm.

For a moment he stood still, looking down at her hand on the fine cloth of his jacket. Then he turned, obviously not wanting in her sympathy.

'Come on. It's time to take our seats.'

CHAPTER TEN

RAFE sat at the conference table, watching an audio-
visual presentation. He hadn't taken in a single fact.
He'd been on edge all day. All night. He hadn't slept
since leaving Antonia's room last night.

A month since they'd become lovers and still the
novelty hadn't worn off. She was endlessly fascinating. Far more so than this presentation.

If he wasn't careful she'd distract him from his
scheme for revenge. That would be disastrous. It was
past time his father paid for his sins.

Yet all day his thoughts had centred on the woman
he'd left curled in bed. She was an intriguing mix
of vamp and innocent. That first night it had been
patently obvious she wasn't as sexually experienced
as he'd assumed, though she had the sensual power
to rob him of coherent thought.

She was a riddle: the woman who grabbed every
penny she could and yet was unmoved by diamonds
that cost a fortune. Who was happiest discussing art
history with some ageing expert. The woman who'd

once encouraged Dexter's intimacies and now shrank from him every time they met.

The woman who'd given Rafe the best sex of his life.

Had her initial coldness been an act to pique his curiosity? He sure as hell hoped so. He'd never met a woman who had the power to arouse him so completely or quickly.

Yet memories flashed into his head. Of her soft eyes, wide and wary. Of her taut self-possession. Of the way she'd almost dare him to take her, refusing to initiate intimacy herself. Then his certainty would crumble a little and something like guilt would crack his complacency.

He had no reason for guilt. He'd offered a deal and she'd taken it. A business transaction and a mutual pleasure. She couldn't deny that. So often he brought her to the brink of ecstasy, then waited till she begged for completion. He needed to hear her husky-voiced pleas, see the stunned delight in her dark eyes, knowing that no other man had ever satisfied her the way he did.

Their first time together had been spectacular. He'd been so aroused just by the sight of her stripping, and then by the feel of her velvet-soft skin against his, that he'd climaxed almost straight away. But to his amazement that excitement had never faded. Each time was like the first. Better, even, as he learned what pleased her most, so she became willing and wanton in his arms.

Last night he'd wanted to stay with her, wrapped in her sleek warmth, caressed by her long silky hair, hearing the soft sound of her breathing, reliving the ecstasy of their coming together. Anticipating the next time.

Yet in the afterglow of sexual satisfaction he'd read danger. He could so easily be tempted to spend even more time with her. Already she stole his attention when, as now, he had important business to attend to.

No, she had her place in his life—temporarily. It would be unwise to give her more. He sat straighter, resolving to concentrate on the presentation.

A few minutes later he glanced at his watch, calculating how long before he could wrap up his meeting.

Rafe arrived home early. She'd be getting ready. He couldn't remember where they were going. Some reception where he could remind his father that he, Rafe, possessed the woman the older man wanted. Each hungry, frustrated stare Stuart Dexter directed at Antonia was balm to Rafe's soul. Revenge was sweet and it could only get better.

Perhaps she was in the shower. His thoughts strayed to an image of water sluicing lovingly over each curve, of it sliding down the perfection of those long, long legs.

His body grew taut. He flung his briefcase onto

a side table, tugged his coat from his shoulders and threw it onto a sofa, then strode down the hall.

He found her in the bathroom, her back to him. She was fully clothed, but the sight of her pulled him up short. His breath punched from his body as shock rippled through him.

Impossible that she could go *anywhere* dressed like that. Yet she could wear it for him any time—privately. He'd revel in watching her. For the few minutes before he stripped her naked.

His gaze trawled down sleek black leather, fitted like a glove over her narrow shoulders and even narrower waist. The flare of her hips was accentuated by the wide belt she wore over tight-fitting leather trousers. Rafe eyed the perfect curve of her buttocks, searching for evidence of underwear but finding none. Heat shot to his groin.

Her legs looked impossibly long and sexy. Once again she was wearing heels so high she looked like a...

A mistress, he realised as she met his gaze in the wide mirror. A very expensive, very sexy mistress.

She'd done something to her eyes, darkening them. They looked exotic and blatantly sensual. Her lips were red, glossy, a pout straight from one of his erotic dreams. Around her throat was a narrow ribbon of black velvet that emphasised the pure, delicate line of her throat and managed to draw attention down to the zip of her jacket, undone just enough to hint at the inviting abundance below.

His libido roared into full gear.

He read some fleeting expression in her eyes. Surprise perhaps, but then the blankness he'd come to hate shuttered it. He'd never met a woman so controlled, so apparently impervious to him—at least until he got her naked.

'You're home early.' She didn't even turn to face him, much less offer a greeting.

Rafe wondered if he should renegotiate their contract. How much would he have to pay to get a welcome kiss when he came home? Though maybe wives did that, not mistresses.

'My meetings ended earlier than expected.' Because he'd cancelled the last one, eager to get back and see her.

'Then you'll have plenty of time to get ready for tonight.' She turned her attention to the mascara she was applying, dismissing him.

But Rafe wasn't a man to be dismissed. He paced forward till he was flush behind her. She froze, then slowly lifted the mascara wand to her face.

He put his hand on her buttock and felt her stiffen. Warm leather, soft female, and nothing, he'd swear, between them. The realisation sparked all sorts of salacious thoughts. He slid his hand down, enjoying the knowledge that she was his for the taking. This delicious, tantalising witch of a woman was his alone. She was one hell of a temptress.

'That's a sexy new outfit,' he murmured, swaying forward to shadow her body. 'Did you buy it to celebrate?' A month of mind-blowing sex was an excellent reason to party. He especially approved of the gift wrapping. He eyed the zip of her jacket, with its tantalisingly large tab.

'Celebrate?' She looked at him in the mirror, her eyes wide and questioning. 'Is this some special occasion?'

Rafe's mouth firmed as he watched her expression of apparent confusion. She knew what he was talking about. He could read the knowledge in her oh-so-innocent look.

He shrugged, noting how her eyes fixed on the rise of his shoulders in the mirror. She tried to hide the fact, but Antonia was as fascinated by him as he was by her.

'Not particularly.' He lowered his other hand to cup her bottom, squeezing gently till she squirmed and put down the mascara. She felt so good. His fingers massaged the backs of her thighs then slid higher again. Oh, yes!

'It's almost a shame that I'm the only man who'll ever see you in this.' He leaned forward to nip her on the nape. His hands slid round her hips and arrowed down to the V of her legs, to the heat there. He nudged her legs apart with his thigh, planting himself intimately close.

'But I'm wearing it tonight,' she protested.

Slowly he shook his head. 'Absolutely not.' He lifted one hand to her jacket zip and tugged, exposing her bra and bare torso. 'If you went out in that you'd cause a riot.'

She swatted at his hand, yanking the zip back up. 'But I'm already dressed.' Flashing dark eyes met his in the wide mirror and he felt a surge of excitement, as he always did when they argued.

'Then you can just get *undressed*.' He lifted his hands to the back zip of her trousers and eased it down, enjoying the view of her naked cheeks. He'd been mistaken. She was wearing a tiny wisp of a thong. He hooked a finger underneath it and traced her bare flesh, enjoying the tremor she couldn't hide.

Urgently now, he shoved her leather pants down, then reached round to tug her jacket undone. It was the work of a moment to undo the front catch of her bra so her unbound breasts spilled into his waiting palms. He pressed himself against her backside, his erection pushing against her. Scorching heat roared through his bloodstream.

Soon, very soon, he'd be inside her. He surged close, tilting his hips forward, anticipating his release. In the mirror he watched his tanned fingers massage the ultra-soft skin on the underside of her pale breasts. There was something about the sight of her naked flesh against his that was incredibly erotic. He could barely wait. He fished a condom from his pocket.

Quickly he released his trousers and tore the packet.

'Are you sure you want to do this now?' Antonia's voice was cool. 'You don't want to be late tonight, do you? I thought it was some important event we were going to.'

Rafe paused, meeting her eyes, reading the veneer of boredom in her expression. With her raised eyebrows, the angled chin, her nostrils flaring as if in distaste, she was the picture of suffering patience.

In contrast, he was randy as a teenager, his need urgent and unbridled. Yet Antonia was apparently unmoved. Damn it, she was doing it again—distancing herself, pretending she had no interest in sex, or in him. Each night he had to break down that brittle shell to the passionate woman she hid so well.

His mind filled with the image of him standing behind her, pushing her forward so she was fully exposed to him. He'd thrust into her depths till he was sated, her breasts cupped in his hands, his lips on the soft skin of her neck. Completion would be swift and glorious. But it would end with her looking down her supercilious nose at him.

She was deliberately goading him. As if she *wanted* him to find his pleasure without her. As if she didn't want to sully herself with anything as honest as lust.

'Not as important as this, lover.' He spun her round to face him, enjoying her surprise. Then he bent down, dragging off her shoes and tugging at the tight trousers till finally he'd wrestled the leather away from her.

'Now, where were we?' He enjoyed the flash of near panic on her face as he yanked off her belt, then slid her jacket fully open. He reached down to the scrap of fabric covering the juncture of her thighs. The slight ripping sound as he tore it away was loud in the quiet room.

'Ah, that's right. *Here*, I think.' He slipped a finger down between her legs, unerringly finding the sensitive bud he sought.

A quiver rippled through her, but she stood stock still. He probed further, delving inside, then stroking out again, again and again, until he felt the sway of her lower body pushing into his touch. No mistaking her arousal now. The scent of feminine musk teased his nostrils, urging him on. He lowered his head to her breast and was rewarded with a gasp of delight.

By the time he straightened her eyes were glazed, hot and feverish under heavy lids. This was how he wanted her. Warm and wanton and ready. He hoisted her up onto the wide bench below the mirror.

'Lift your legs,' he ordered.

As soon as her thighs closed around his hips he positioned himself against her, then pushed deep inside till he was anchored at her very core.

Antonia blinked, trying to clear her eyes of excess moisture. She couldn't believe it had happened again. Each time she steeled herself to resist, reminding herself that it was just sex. Crude, unvarnished physical lust. Yet each time she caved in, giving herself up to the magic of Rafe's touch as if afraid she'd never experience it again.

Aftershocks of pleasure rippled through her and she sank bonelessly into Rafe's hard torso, grateful for his arms holding her tight as she came back down to earth.

No matter how often she told herself she despised him, he still overcame her resolve with just a few caresses, or that sultry low murmur of his voice as he whispered outrageous suggestions in her ear.

Where was her backbone? Bad enough that she'd sold herself as his mistress. Did she have to enjoy her own downfall quite so much? Hot distress filled her.

Pride demanded that she remain unmoved, yet Rafe could bend her to his will with shaming ease.

She'd thought tonight at least she'd stand firm. She'd woken this morning to realise she'd shared herself with him for precisely a month. The knowledge had left a bitter taste in her mouth.

Tonight's outfit had been another gesture of defiance. Futile, perhaps, but important to her—a sign of her autonomy. She spent her time pandering to his whims, ignoring the pointed jibes of people who saw her as fair game now she was so obviously Rafe's possession. People who knew what it meant when she wore his glittering jewels yet obviously didn't hold his affection. For he never pretended she was anything more than a convenient companion.

Antonia had lost count of the questions about the size of her allowance. And the lewd suggestions from men wanting to offer her a *private arrangement* when Rafe tired of her.

Her self-respect had been shattered and her pride tarnished. She bluffed her way through by pretending to an insouciance she didn't feel. Yet inside she felt stripped to the bone. Her soul shrivelled every time she had to face those knowing looks and lascivious stares.

What would her parents have said if they'd known what she did for their sakes? They'd have been horrified.

But she'd saved what was really important: her father's memory and her mother's charity. She'd heard from Emma at the Foundation that the auditors had found some unusual transactions, but that officially no further action was being taken since the money was there and her father's access code was no longer valid.

So it was all worthwhile. She had to believe that.

'Hold on tight.' Antonia felt Rafe's words against the side of her neck as he lifted her up in his embrace. Automatically she held on till they reached the bed and fell together onto its wide expanse.

Still he didn't release her.

'I'll go and find something else to wear,' she said, eyes fixed on his squared chin just a few inches away.

'No.'

'No?' Startled, she raised her eyes to his. His gaze was intent, his brow furrowed, as if he tried to solve a knotty problem.

'No. We're staying here. And I'm going to make long, slow love to you until you forget how to scowl.' He lifted his hand to her face, his touch infinitely gentle, not at all like the ruthless man who'd just stripped her in the bathroom. Or the man who walked away from her each night after she'd given him what he wanted.

Antonia felt his fingers slide along her brow, smoothing the lines of her frown. His other hand caressed her cheek in a slow motion that felt like tenderness.

'But I—'

'No buts, Antonia. You don't want to go out tonight, do you?'

Helplessly she gazed up at him, fearing he could read far more in her face than she could in his. But for once the determination that had held her steadfast these past weeks had drained away, leaving her tired and vulnerable.

Of course she didn't want to go out. She was the envy of a lot of women, yet it grew harder each day to overcome her sense of shame, of failure, that she hadn't been able to find another way to protect her family.

Worse still was the guilty knowledge that she enjoyed the perks of her position far too much. If she wasn't careful she'd become addicted to the feel of his strong arms round her, to the sound of his lazy drawl when he made love to her.

Then where would she be, when the time came to go her own way? She should be focusing on her plans for the future, not his impressive lovemaking.

She shook her head.

'Good.' His mouth curved up in a thoughtful smile that made her heart beat faster.

His lips closed on hers, coaxing a response with their slow, luxurious caress. It felt as if he had all the time in the world and nothing on his mind except her. If she believed in fairy tales she'd even be tempted to think he cared, just a little.

Antonia's last coherent thought before she succumbed to his slow seduction was to wish she was gullible enough to believe it would all turn out right in the end.

CHAPTER ELEVEN

THAT was the night everything began to change.

The differences were so subtle that sometimes Antonia wondered if she imagined them. Despite her attempts to remain aloof, they seemed to be building a relationship.

A flush warmed her cheeks now, as she hurried through the lunchtime crowd. Sex was still a vital part of what they shared. Each day her inhibitions dissolved further as he teased and tempted as well as demanded. Rafe had an uninhibited sensuality, and a generosity when it came to sharing pleasure that was fast destroying her defences.

Yet there was a sense of growing closeness, of a sharing more intimate than physical caresses.

That evening when he'd taken her hard and fast in the bathroom had been the first time he'd stayed the night with her. She'd woken at dawn in the warm cocoon of his arms. Her sense of wellbeing and contentment had been a revelation. It had felt different between them, as if this time he'd shared something more than the hard perfection of his body and his erotic expertise. Something of himself.

After the lacerating pain of those earlier nights, watching him leave her room, she hadn't been able to help reading significance into his decision to share her bed. It was as if he took comfort in her company, as she did in his, especially in the early hours when grief had previously kept her awake and hurting.

Now he spent every night with her, holding her close, giving her the solace she'd so long desired. Under his tender ministrations the ice around her heart had begun to fracture and thaw, just a little.

Rafe even *sounded* different. He was less ready to jump to negative conclusions. He listened more, and she sometimes found him watching her with a curious expression that made her wonder what he found so fascinating.

They went out less, often spending a night in with a meal he had ordered and a fine bottle of wine. They'd chat about almost anything: travel, movies, politics. Afterwards Rafe would say he needed to work, but somehow he'd never open his laptop and they'd end up in each other's arms.

Even when they went out, to some grand dinner or elegant soirée, there was a change. No longer did she feel like a trophy, cold-bloodedly displayed to complement Rafe's power and prestige. Instead he introduced her to people he thought might interest her, especially those with an interest in art. She'd discovered Rafe Benton could be charming, attentive, witty—the sort of man she'd *choose* to spend time with.

He'd even steered her clear of Stuart Dexter more than once, since she'd let slip how much she disliked the man. Rafe's brows had risen, and for a moment he'd looked doubtful, but from then on she'd seen far less of Dexter.

If Antonia wasn't careful she'd find herself liking this new Rafe far too much.

She was smiling as she turned in to the cosy Italian restaurant. She knew she shouldn't set too much store by the change in him, in *them*. Yet after the pain of the last months her bruised soul responded to his warmth, his wit, his tenderness, with a yearning she couldn't repress.

'Antonia.' Suddenly he was there, and her heart flipped over at the impact of his rare smile. He was so handsome, and more charismatic than any man she'd ever met.

Her hand trembled as he lifted it to his lips. Blue eyes fixed on hers as he turned her hand over and pressed his mouth to the underside of her wrist. His tongue, erotically inviting, ran over the sensitive pulse point and tendrils of desire instantly wove round her.

'Rafe!' She tugged her hand away, afraid that she'd melt into a puddle of longing right there in the restaurant.

The glint in his eyes told her he knew precisely the effect he had on her. His hand was possessive at her back as he steered her to their table. Strangely, she didn't mind that proprietorial gesture nearly as much as she once had.

'I approve of the skirt,' he said as he sat beside her in a secluded booth. Underneath the table he planted his hand on her knee, pulling up the fabric till his broad palm touched sheer stockings. Antonia shivered at the pleasurable sensations that radiated in whorls of heat from his touch.

'Rafe, no. Someone will see,' she hissed.

His lazy smile as he stroked her inner thigh was deliciously wicked, reminding her of the way they'd spent the night, locked in each other's embrace. She wished they had more than just this lunchtime gap between his meetings.

'Please,' she said. 'Not here.'

'No?' he teased. With one final caress, he smoothed her skirt and lifted his hand to close around hers on the table. Any bystander would look at them and think they were a couple in love.

With a sudden pang Antonia wondered exactly what it was Rafe felt for her. Something more than lust, she was sure. The question haunted her days.

She shied away from examining her own feelings. They were far too complicated, and her innate sense of self-preservation warned against delving.

Surely these confused emotions were a good reason to concentrate on planning her future? In a few months she'd be a free agent, able to pursue those dreams she'd put on hold while she looked

after her father. She'd work as a guide till she could
start the Art History course she'd set her heart on,
and then find a permanent job and a little place of
her own somewhere.

Why didn't the idea seem as appealing as it used
to?

'Are you hungry?' Rafe asked. His knowing
gleam told her he wasn't just talking about food.
His smile scrambled her thoughts.

She nodded. 'I'm always hungry when I come
here. It has the best Italian food in London.'

He raised his brows.

'Really. It's marvellous.' It had been her mother's
favourite restaurant, and she cherished memories of
it.

'Antonia! *Ragazza mia bella! Come stai? Dove
sei stata?*' Antonia looked up into familiar coal dark
eyes and felt a grin spread across her face.

'Domenico!' She let herself be drawn up into
brawny arms, blinking back sudden tears. Domenico
was the owner and head waiter, someone she'd
known since birth. He was a big man, and his bear
hug squeezed her breathless. It was a sensation that
took her straight back to her childhood.

'*Sto bene. E tu, Domenico?*'

'*Cosi cosi,*' he answered, gesturing with his flat
hand and chuckling.

Rafe listened to the rapid exchange in Italian.
Another facet of his lover he hadn't known about.

She really was a mystery. He'd never known a woman so close-lipped about herself.

As he watched the older man hug her tight, and saw her laughing response to something he'd said, Rafe knew a sudden, unprecedented surge of envy. Antonia never looked at *him* like that, with her expression utterly unshadowed.

Even in the throes of passion she held something of herself back. He'd barely tapped into her secrets. Secrets that each day it seemed increasingly important for him to uncover.

Now she glowed with joy. The sight of her radiant beauty stole his breath. Antonia had always been lovely, even when she put on the ice queen act or tried his temper with her provocative attitude. Now he saw her bone-deep beauty. The sun itself seemed to shine from her smile.

He wanted that look for himself.

'Aren't you going to introduce me?' he said, getting to his feet and slipping a possessive arm around her.

She turned, and the warmth of her smile slid through him, deep into his chest.

'Rafe, this is Domenico Licarta, a friend of my parents. Domenico, this is Rafe Benton.'

'Mr Benton, it's good to meet you. I see you're looking after our Antonia. It's been a difficult time for her.' His grizzled eyebrows drew together as he turned to her. 'I was so sorry to hear about your father.'

Antonia nodded, her lips pursed in a wobbly line. 'It was sudden.' Her voice was husky with emotion. 'He'd had bad news from the cardiologist. Worse, I think, than he let on... You know what he was like.'

Her voice trailed off and Rafe watched her swallow jerkily, her eyes over-bright.

'At least this way it was quick,' she said. 'I don't think he could have coped with becoming an invalid.'

Rafe's arm tightened, drawing her close. Something punched low in his belly at that hitch in her voice. He barely listened to Domenico's murmurs of condolence as he absorbed the evidence of Antonia's grief. There was no mistaking it. He was all too familiar with the anguish of loss after the death of his mother.

Rafe frowned, remembering her hard-as-nails composure in Switzerland, the comments he'd overheard about her aloofness, and his conviction that she was too cold-blooded to experience true sorrow at the loss of her father.

Yet he could feel it now in her taut frame, in the tiny tremors running through her body as he held her against him. Each breath she dragged in was just a little unsteady as she smiled crookedly at the big, concerned Italian.

Rafe experienced a jolt of dismay. Had he been so arrogant, so wrapped up in his own plans for revenge, that he hadn't looked properly? Hadn't read the grief behind the icily composed face she presented to the world?

Hell! If he'd missed that, what else had he missed?

'Sit, sit.' Their host was gesturing to their booth seat. 'No need for a menu. I'll bring you a special meal. Only the best for my little Antonia and her friend.'

Snapping dark eyes met his from under beetling brows, and Rafe knew the Italian was taking his measure.

'Thank you. Antonia has been telling me you have the best food in London.' He pulled her down beside him, taking her cool hand in his, automatically chafing it warm.

The other man nodded, accepting the compliment as his due, then with one final inquisitive glance bustled off towards the kitchens.

'You have a fan,' Rafe murmured, watching her drawn face closely. It was a relief to see her lips curve up in a smile and know he'd coaxed it from her.

'Actually, Domenico was a fan of my mother's.'

'Really?'

She nodded and gestured to a wall. It was covered with pictures of famous guests, all flanked by a smiling Domenico and others whom Rafe guessed were family members.

'That one in the centre, third row down.' She pointed to a portrait of a dark-haired woman with a face that would stop traffic. 'That's my mother, Claudia Benzoni.'

'The actress?' Rafe had seen some of her films, though they'd been made when he was just a kid. The experts called them classics of Italian cinema. In his youthful enthusiasm he'd been too busy appreciating the female star to notice their artistic significance.

'That's right.' No mistaking the warmth in Antonia's voice. Or the wistfulness.

Rafe remembered hearing about the actress's untimely death from a rare form of cancer years ago. It had stuck in his mind because it had happened about the time his own mother's illness had taken another turn for the worse.

'She was beautiful,' he said. 'Almost as lovely as you.'

Antonia turned, her expression astonished. He took in her large eyes, her lush mouth, her classic beauty, and felt something tug deep inside him. A need to banish the shadows from her eyes.

Rafe put his finger under her chin, revelling in the soft texture of her flesh, and tilted her face up. He leaned forward and pressed a slow, tender kiss to her lips.

When Rafe kissed her like that, Antonia's mind ceased to function. Instead she was simply *aware*. Of him, of the steady acceleration of her pulse as desire built, and of a warmth that was more of the spirit than the body.

How could that be, when their relationship was based on sex? It was at times like this she felt something significant developing between them. Rafe was fast becoming important to her.

He broke the kiss and she stared dazedly into eyes the colour of heaven. When he smiled at her so intimately, his lips tilting up in a little twist of shared pleasure—

'Here you are,' Domenico boomed as he strode to the table. 'The best *stracciatella* outside Italy. I guarantee it.' He placed two steaming bowls on the table and stood back, grinning in anticipation.

Hastily Antonia sat back in her seat, flushed at being caught out, so absorbed in Rafe's kiss.

'Thank you, Domenico. It's my favourite.'

He nodded. 'Of course. You think I'd forget?' He looked across at Rafe. 'Try it. You've never tasted anything like Mamma's *stracciatella*.'

Antonia picked up her spoon and leaned close to the aromatic dish. Instantly memories flooded her. She took a spoonful and closed her eyes for a moment. Heaven!

'As good as ever, Domenico! Wonderful.' She looked at Rafe, apparently hesitant beside her. 'Try it,' she urged.

She watched Rafe taste the soup, then swallow, the movement of his strong, corded neck fascinating her. Whatever was happening to her, it was serious if she found herself diverted just by the sight of the man eating!

'Antonia's right.' Rafe nodded his appreciation.

'You sound surprised,' Antonia ventured as Domenico moved away to serve another table.

'I don't like soup,' he said. 'But this is better than most.' He spooned up another mouthful.

Antonia frowned. She knew people who disliked the taste of various foods, but a dislike of soup? Intriguing.

'That's…unusual,' she ventured.

Rafe shrugged. 'When for years it's virtually all you have to eat, it begins to pall.'

'Were you sick? Did you need a light diet?' Antonia found it hard to imagine him as anything but superbly fit. But he never spoke of the past, only the present.

'No, it was simply our staple diet. Nutritious, easy to prepare, and very, very cheap,' he said, his voice holding a bitter note.

Antonia frowned at his words. His family had been short of cash?

He caught her staring. 'You find that surprising?'

'I… Well, I suppose I'd assumed your family was well off.' After all, he was so supremely confident of his power, arrogantly at ease with his extreme wealth. He seemed like a man born to money.

Rafe smiled, a brief twist of the lips that reminded her of the hard derision that had been so obvious in him when they'd met.

'Born with a silver spoon in my mouth?' He shook

his head. 'Anything but.' He sat back in his chair. 'There was just me and my mother. She was good at what she did—she was an executive assistant—but it was hard finding a job that gave her time to bring up a child too. She settled for one with flexible hours, but the downside was lower pay. It was always a struggle.'

'Your father didn't contribute?' She supposed she shouldn't pry, but it was so rare for him to open up about his past she couldn't prevent the question.

'My *father*?' No mistaking the dismissal in *that* tone, or the seething flare of emotion in Rafe's blazing eyes. 'He washed his hands of us before I was born. He didn't give a damn if we lived in poverty. Or even if we lived.'

Antonia stiffened, shocked at his words and by the rabid loathing she heard. Surely Rafe was exaggerating? But as she saw the expressions flit across his granite features, his mouth compress into a forbidding line, she realised he was speaking the truth as he saw it.

What sort of man could be so unfeeling towards his own flesh and blood? Antonia's parents had been deeply in love and had shared that love with her. How lucky she'd been.

'It must have been hard on one salary,' she murmured.

Rafe raised his eyebrows. 'Lots of families manage on one wage,' he said. 'Our problem was that my mother couldn't keep her job, not full-time. She was diagnosed with a degenerative illness.'

He thrust a hand through his dark hair in a gesture that hinted at uncharacteristic vulnerability and made Antonia want to reach out to him.

'She fought it every step of the way, but it was rough going. Even before she was confined to a wheelchair she was often too exhausted or sick to work. There was a never-ending barrage of medical bills on top of everything else.'

'How did you manage?' Antonia was appalled that she'd inadvertently blundered into such a painful memories.

Rafe shrugged. As she watched his expensively tailored jacket pull tight over those wide shoulders, Antonia wondered about the innate strength and determination that had got him to the very pinnacle of the business world.

'Any way we could. I held down a string of jobs even as a kid. We grew our own produce, and I became an expert at making ends meet.' He shook his head. 'One of the first things I did when I started making real money was take her out for the best steak and seafood meal I could afford. I still remember the taste of it.'

Antonia's fingers closed around his sleeve. 'You don't have to…' She gestured to his bowl.

'What? I don't have to finish my soup?' The brooding intensity of his expression was banished by an unexpected flash of humour. 'It's okay, Antonia.

I'm not so damaged by my past that I can't manage a bowl of the stuff.' His gaze held hers for so long his smile faded and his expression slid back into taut lines. 'Right now I'm more interested in knowing how I came to tell you all this.'

He looked truly discomfited by the extent to which he'd opened up about his childhood. She guessed he'd view the sharing of personal information as a weakness.

'Perhaps I'm a good listener?' She tried to lighten the atmosphere.

'Perhaps.'

He reached out and cupped her chin in his hand, staring into her eyes. The intensity of his regard warmed her right to the core, just as his touch heated her skin. This close, she felt she could almost drown in the cerulean depths of that compelling gaze.

'Or,' he murmured in that low, rough suede tone that always sent a shiver through her, 'perhaps you're a witch.'

They spent the rest of the meal ostensibly concentrating on the superb food. They spoke little, yet to Antonia it seemed that their silences were companionable.

Between courses Rafe pulled her in close against his solid warmth and asked about her own childhood. What had it been like growing up with an Italian movie starlet for a mother? Where had they lived?

Antonia told him about her early years, surprised

to discover how easy it was to talk with him. It was good to relive the memories, as if by recalling them she affirmed the importance of the parents she'd lost.

By the time they'd finished their meal and were drinking coffee Antonia was replete and relaxed. She refused to think about anything other than the comforting feel of Rafe's arm around her and the sound of his voice, deep enough to burr her skin into gooseflesh.

She felt so good. Better than she'd felt in a long, long time. Even before her father's accident she'd felt as if she was spinning frantically on a wheel, working when she could to supplement their income, but worrying when she was away from him, for his heart condition and his mood swings had concerned her. Then, at the resort, with Stuart Dexter hanging around and her fear for her father notching up by the day, she'd been on tenterhooks.

'Ready to go?' Rafe asked.

Reluctantly she nodded and gathered her bag. She'd prefer to stay here all afternoon, but it wasn't possible.

It was late by the time they were out on the pavement, after saying their farewells to Domenico and his family, and promising to return soon.

Antonia frowned at her watch. 'I didn't realise we'd be so long. Do you have meetings this afternoon?'

'Nothing that can't be deferred,' he said, 'for something more important.'

She tilted her head questioningly. 'More important?'

'Yes.' Slowly his mouth curved into a smile. The full force of it weakened her knees. 'I can think of several things I'd rather do—if you're agreeable.'

The glint in his eyes was easy to read. Rafe was thinking about the two of them naked. The realisation sent a rush of liquid heat through her.

'But your meetings…' She'd learned in these past weeks that *nothing* was more important to Rafe than his current business project. It was all-consuming.

'It can wait.' He paused. 'If you want.'

Antonia had never heard Rafe sound hesitant. But there was no mistaking the question in his expression, or the waiting stillness of his big frame.

He was asking if she wanted intimacy. *Asking.*

Previously, even when he'd coaxed, teased or dared her into sex, *he'd* made the decision and had acted on it.

Now the decision was hers.

Was it stupid to feel that this was somehow momentous? Surely she was reading too much into it? Nevertheless, she felt far more than physical desire, more than anticipation, as she slipped her arm through his and whispered, 'Yes'.

Fifteen minutes later they were in a fourth-floor bedroom in the nearest hotel. Rafe had called his office to cancel his meetings while he strode down the street at a fast clip, shepherding her along beside him as if he had to keep her close. He'd organised a room in record time, and once they were alone divested them both of their clothes with a speed that left her breathless and excited.

The urgency of his actions, the intensity of his expression as his hands swept over her, stole her breath. She wondered if they'd even make it to the bed.

Yet once he yanked the coverlet away, and they were lying on crisp linen sheets, Rafe slowed. The urgency was still there. She could sense it in his rough breathing, the heavy thud of his pulse and the fine tremor of his hands. It was an urgency that matched her own. She shifted, restless and wanting, stroking her palms over him, clutching him close, wanting more. Needing *him*.

He had other plans. For long minutes—for hours, it seemed—Rafe stroked, kissed, nipped, and caressed the whole of her, from her face to her feet. He brought her to the brink of completion again and again, and then moved on to pleasure her elsewhere.

Never had she reached such a fever-pitch of desire. He was so focused on her: her pleasure, her responses, her needs. She felt a connection with him as never before.

At last he gave in to her hoarse pleas and positioned himself above her. Antonia looked into his face: proud, tense with restraint, yet so tender. She felt the hard knot inside that she'd lived with for so long melt and ease.

She felt whole.

With a single slow surge of power he brought them together. Antonia opened for him, taking him deep inside, revelling in the ecstasy that was already welling up and exploding through her.

'Rafe! I...' Her words died and she hung on tight to his slick, powerful body as they moved together. He was her reality, her world, her safety net. Everything spun away into glorious, mind-numbing bliss.

It was only much later, as she lay wrapped close in his arms, the fuzz of his chest hair under her cheek, his broad palm splayed possessively on her hip, that Antonia realised what it was she'd been going to say.

Rafe. I love you.

CHAPTER TWELVE

'YOU like it?'

Antonia stared at the small box Rafe had just pressed into her hands and blinked back absurd tears. The brooch was gorgeous. Elegant, stylish, and so *her*. She stroked the silver, noting the loving detail in the small artist's palette and brush.

'It's lovely. Absolutely perfect,' she murmured.

How different from the diamonds he'd bought her. This was another one-off piece, designed by a master. Yet it had been chosen for *her*. It wasn't gaudy glitter obtained solely to show off Rafe's bought woman.

Antonia's chest squeezed tight as warmth trickled through her, filling even those places in her guarded heart that had remained frozen until now.

'Why did you—?'

'It reminded me of you,' he answered, his voice an intimately soft rumble. 'I saw it and I had to have it for you. Here, let me.' He took the piece from her.

She looked up, noting the way his brows crinkled in concentration. The firm line of his jaw that only a few hours ago had rubbed against her cheek as they'd made long, slow love in the dawn light. The fan of dark eyelashes that hid his eyes as he looked down.

After three months Rafe's face was so familiar. So dear. She couldn't prevent the welling tenderness as she stared up into those features she'd once thought so hard.

Now she knew another side of him. Her lover could be a generous, protective, caring man. He made her forget that he'd pushed her into intimacy as part of a business arrangement. Their relationship felt like anything *but* business. She'd even started hoping that one day he might reciprocate her feelings. The love that had at first so terrified her and now was her secret delight.

She wasn't mistaken. He felt *something* for her. She knew he did. Could it ever be love? Was she fooling herself, dreaming they had a chance of happiness?

Inevitably her mind shifted to the tiny changes she'd noticed recently. The slight tenderness in her breasts, the delay in her monthly cycle. They meant nothing...probably. They'd been so careful—though she knew these things could happen... A whisper of excitement shivered through her. What if Rafe really did care? And what if...?

'There. Perfect.' Dazzling bright eyes met hers, and a shaft of heat pierced her heart.

'Aren't you going to look?' Despite his light tone, his expression was serious, intent.

Hope surged and she forgot her doubts, for now.

'It's stunning,' she said as she turned to the mirror. Antonia lifted a hand and stroked the metal tentatively.

'I'll treasure it.' *Always* she added silently. 'Thank you, Rafe.'

'It was entirely my pleasure.'

The sight of his tall frame beside hers and the glimmer of approval in his eyes filled her with delight. *Yes*. Surely she was right and he felt this spark between them?

'I thought it would appeal to your artistic soul.'

Rafe met her look in the mirror and felt a punch to the abdomen. The sight of her smiling at him like that, so open, so radiant, did the strangest things. He'd been jealous of those smiles that day she'd directed them at Domenico Licarta. Now he had them for himself. He felt a greedy delight that told him it would be a long time before he tired of Antonia.

The six months he'd arranged with her wouldn't be enough. Maybe he'd invite her to holiday in Australia after his business here was complete.

He lifted a hand and stroked his knuckles down her cheek. Inevitably the contact sent desire swirling through him. No matter that they'd just spent the night and half the morning together naked. He couldn't get enough of her.

'Have you ever done any painting yourself?' He slipped in the question, needing to divert his thoughts lest they end up in the hotel's king-sized bed again.

He had a specific reason for bringing Antonia on a weekend in the country. But first they had to make it out of their room!

She shook her head, and her hair swirled around her shoulders, loose and inviting, just the way he liked it.

'I tried, but I have no talent. Just enough of an eye to begin appreciating what I see.' She stroked the brooch gently, as if it were a living thing. 'I plan to enrol in an Art History degree one day. Then, if I'm lucky, I'll get a job in a museum or a gallery, or an auction house.'

Rafe stared. A job? More than that—a job in a field that, from the little he knew, was difficult to break into. One that required years of dedicated study.

He frowned. She'd never mentioned a career. He'd thought she was content to live off the allowance her family had no doubt left her. If she wanted to supplement her income, surely there was something easier, especially with her looks?

'Is this a new idea?'

'No.' She shook her head and her cloud of dark hair slid round her, its fresh scent filling his nostrils. 'It's what I've always wanted.'

'So why have you left it so long?'

Her hand dropped from the brooch. 'My father needed me. He was sick and lonely, despite all his socialising. He needed someone to look after him. There was only me.'

Abruptly she turned, and walked across the room to where her coat and bag lay on the end of the bed.

'Are you ready to leave?'

Rafe's eyes narrowed. She was changing the subject. Because he'd reminded her of her grief, or because she was lying? But why lie? Antonia had always been up-front. She didn't shy from confrontation, and she'd never hidden her blatant interest in his cash.

Yet the woman he'd got to know wasn't simply the grasping siren he'd pegged her for. She was far more complex.

Who was she? In some ways she was still an enigma. He wished he'd taken the time to find out at the beginning instead of focusing all his energies on revenge.

'Yes, I'm ready.' He thrust the puzzle from his mind, vowing to revisit it soon.

'I know this place!' The sight of a long formal carriageway tugged Antonia from her pleasant haze. Drifts of daffodils, rows of huge elms, and in the distance a glimpse of the rhododendron garden to one end of a lake.

Every year the Claudia Benzoni Foundation's gala charity lunch was hosted here, in one of Britain's loveliest privately owned heritage homes. She'd received her invitation weeks ago, but hadn't for a moment supposed she'd be able to get away from London to attend.

Rafe glanced at her briefly before he changed gear to guide the sports car over an ornamental bridge.

'I thought you'd want to attend the fundraiser for your mother's charity.' He paused. 'Why didn't you tell me about it? I only found out when I received an invitation.'

Antonia shrugged. 'I assumed you wouldn't leave London for something that wasn't…relevant to your business. I know how important your work is.' Nor had she imagined he'd be happy for her to come alone. Rafe wanted her near.

His mouth pursed at her words, as if she'd said the wrong thing. But it was true. He was single-minded about his business, except lately, when she'd dared to dream there might be something else occupying his thoughts.

'You could have asked.'

'Thank you, Rafe.' Tentatively she touched his arm. 'I appreciate you bringing me here.' She'd been sad at the prospect of missing the event, which had always been a high point for her and her father. 'It was thoughtful of you.'

More than thoughtful. It was a wonderful surprise.

He flashed her another quick glance, then lifted one hand off the wheel to close over hers, clamping her hand against his taut muscles.

'My pleasure, lover.' His expression was pure

male speculation. 'I'll look forward to your grati-
tude later.'

Antonia smiled at the laughter in his voice even
as answering need burst into life inside her at the
promise in his tone. She loved Rafe's teasing as much
as his blatant desire and his tender gestures.

She glanced out of the window, seeing the carpet
of bulbs and the swelling buds on the trees. Spring
had arrived. Suddenly she realised the arctic grip
around her heart had eased too. The ice-hard barrier
that had kept her apart from the world had melted.

She felt Rafe's touch on her hand and realised she
wasn't alone any more. It felt good.

Hours later, Antonia excused herself and headed
for the restroom. It had been a wonderful day, and
a relief to see the Foundation thriving despite the
near-calamity of the theft. A quiet word with one of
the officials had assured her that Gavin Malleson's
name was safe.

She'd spoken to acquaintances, and some of her
father's friends, and it hadn't been nearly the chore
she'd feared receiving their condolences, for Rafe
had been at her side.

The man was a puzzle. She'd been dumbfounded
when Rafe's name had been announced as a sponsor,
with a pledge for a staggering amount. He'd been
chagrined as applause had swelled through the room,
then he'd shrugged and murmured that it might en-
courage others to donate.

The door to the ladies' room was just ahead when she heard someone approach rapidly from behind.

'Antonia Malleson,' said a voice she knew. 'And without her minder. How unusual!'

Antonia stared up into Stuart Dexter's gaze and felt something like fear chill her blood.

'In here, my dear.'

Before she knew it, he'd swung her round into an open doorway. She wrenched her arm free, tugging away. Too late she realised that had taken her further inside a small sitting room. Dexter was between her and the now closed door.

'What do you want?' She resolved to stand her ground, but as he paced close and she read his salacious expression she found herself backing away.

'What do I want?' His lip curled. 'What I've always wanted. I'm not used to being denied. I almost had you where I wanted you before. But then you found a way to refill the Foundation's coffers and pay your father's debts.' His gaze trawled down her in a leer that made bile rise in her throat.

'Refill the coffers?' Antonia gaped as his meaning sank in. 'It was *you* who took the money! You who made it look like my father had...' Shock made her sway. And relief. *It hadn't been her dad.*

This was the confirmation she'd wanted for so long. But hard on the heels of relief came guilt. Despite her denials there'd been moments when she'd wondered, when she'd doubted her father.

'A temporary embarrassment of funds made it desirable. But it's not something you'll ever be able to prove.' Dexter shrugged, looking totally unmoved. 'I'd intended to use the situation to persuade you that we should spend more *quality* time together. I was going to help you out if you agreed to be a little more accommodating.'

He stretched out a hand and she shoved it away, aghast at what she was hearing.

'Unfortunately business took me away just when I'd hoped—'

'What? To blackmail me into your bed?' Antonia's breath came in ragged gulps and her blood fizzed with adrenaline.

Those cold eyes stripped her bare and she shuddered.

'But my son beat me to it, didn't he?' Dexter's tone was ugly. 'One sniff of his money and you were straight into his bed. No prudish scruples with *him*.'

What? Disbelief hollowed her churning stomach. She stared, dumbfounded, as his words tumbled through her brain.

Dexter took advantage of her shock to step close, crowding her back so she had nowhere to go.

'Your son?' She choked the words out.

'Of course. Didn't Rafe tell you? How remiss of him. He hasn't mentioned it to me either, but I found out and obviously he knows. Why else go into business with his old man?'

Her Rafe? Dexter's son? The idea was laughable.

But she wasn't laughing. She was staring, stricken, into the face before her and seeing physical similarities.

No! It couldn't be true.

But the shape of the head, the angle of the nose, the strong flyaway eyebrows that gave Rafe his fallen angel look… For the first time she recognised them in the man before her. The shock was like a stab to the chest.

'I don't believe it.' She tried to convince herself.

'Believe it,' Stuart Dexter said.

He lunged forward, pinioning her against a bureau while he tugged her jacket from her shoulders, hauling it down to her elbows and hampering her frantic attempts to escape.

'You've no idea how hard it's been to stand on the sidelines, watching him monopolise you.'

'No!' It was a shriek of horror and fear as Antonia realised he had her trapped, his extra body weight working for him as he pawed her. Desperately she fought him. 'Rafe will kill you!'

'No, no.' Stuart mouthed the words against her now bare shoulder, then bit down till she flinched. 'Like father, like son, you know. We can keep this little arrangement in the family. My prospects are looking up. I'll be able to keep you in style once he's finished with you. What do you say?'

Antonia's gorge rose in her throat as his words sank in. He squeezed, groped, tugged at her clothes.

The room lurched around her as her head swam. She grabbed his shoulders and shoved.

This couldn't be happening! She shut her eyes against the sight of his excitement and summoned all her strength to hold him off. His mouth was on her neck. His hands—

'Not an edifying sight,' drawled a dark familiar voice, and abruptly the weight of Dexter's body was removed.

Antonia swayed, finding herself suddenly alone. She snapped open her eyes.

'Rafe!' He was here. Relief weakened her knees and instinctively she reached out, needing his support.

She couldn't believe her eyes when he stood unmoving, glowering, his hands clenching in spasms at his sides. His jaw was locked and fury vibrated from him in waves. She felt as if just one unwise word would make him explode.

Her hand crept to her throat, fingers splaying protectively. What was going on?

Out of the corner of her eye she saw Stuart Dexter stumble to his feet from the sofa where he'd been shoved. He stayed there, out of Rafe's reach, adjusting his tie.

'Rafe?' She stepped towards him and his brows rose. She faltered as she read his gaze, and something slammed shut deep inside her. Antonia had never thought to see him look at her so again.

She drew in a trembling breath and pulled her

jacket into place with shaky hands. Rafe's coldly disapproving gaze ripped her defences bare.

'Sorry, Rafe.' Antonia heard Dexter as if from a distance. 'But I'm only human, and your little love-bird's been casting out lures.' He shrugged his jacket straight. 'You need to talk to her about it. Personally, I'd—'

'I don't give a damn what you'd do,' Rafe said in a voice like crushed glass as he swung round to face Dexter. 'Get out of here now, before I *really* hurt you.'

Over her thundering pulse Antonia heard the deadly intent in his words. She shuddered. Violence was in the air, like the smell of lightning on a stormy summer afternoon. She reached out and steadied herself on the back of a nearby chair.

She'd never seen anything like Rafe's barely bridled fury. It terrified her.

'We were just renewing an old acquaintance.' Dexter's joviality couldn't hide the fear that shook his voice.

Rafe took a single stride towards him and suddenly Dexter was scurrying out through the door, his bravado deserting him in the face of Rafe's glowering wrath.

The lock clicked and Rafe swung round to face her.

Antonia lifted her chin, refusing to be cowed by his terrific scowl. *She* wasn't the one who had to explain herself. Even now she searched for some

sign that Dexter had lied, that Rafe wasn't his son.
But since he'd planted the idea her conviction had
grown with each moment.

Rafe hadn't been straight with her. He'd lied
about his identity. Why? What else didn't she know?
Foreboding filled her. He seemed a stranger once
more.

'You just couldn't keep away from him, could you?
So much for not liking him.' He paced towards her
till his big frame took up all her vision and his heat
encompassed her.

What? Antonia gaped at him. He couldn't believe
that!

'What was he giving you? Cash? Jewels?' Rafe
bit the words out with a savage gnashing of his teeth.
The accusations slammed into her, sharp and deadly
as knives, plunging straight into her heart.

She opened her mouth on a silent gasp of agony
as they hit home and the foolish hopes she'd harboured bled away to nothing. How could he care for
her when he didn't *trust* her? When he believed her
lacking even in common decency?

*She'd wondered what Rafe thought of her. Now
she knew.*

Anguish twisted inside her. She was grateful for
the chair's support. It prevented her crumbling to the
floor.

'Nothing to say, Antonia?' Rafe goaded. 'Are
you so brazen that you didn't think I'd mind shar-

ing? I specified exclusivity in our agreement. Remember?'

There was a crack of sound as Rafe intercepted her palm, just inches from his cheek. The shock of that connection juddered down her arm. His hold was so tight she should feel pain, but the sensation was eclipsed by the jagged agony of her slashed hopes.

Rafe tugged her close till she was flush against him, her breasts brushing him, his thighs surrounding hers. Nausea welled as she realised their intimacy had always been a sham. He wanted her physically, but clearly he despised her, thought she was mercenary and moral-free.

Nothing had changed. How could she ever have thought…?

'Let me go.' Her voice was a raw whisper.

She thought he hadn't heard. Then, finally, he released his death grip. Her arm dropped to her side, her knees buckled, and she crumpled into the chair.

CHAPTER THIRTEEN

RAFE paced, fighting the red mist of rage that had descended the moment he'd walked into the room.

How had he been gullible enough to believe in her?

He'd been a fair way to convincing himself that Antonia wasn't motivated by money. He'd been almost sure...

But obviously that was wishful thinking. She wouldn't have been in Dexter's arms for anything other than the promise of cash.

How long had it been going on?

He thudded his clenched fist down on a broad windowsill at the end of the room.

He'd allowed himself to believe that Antonia was more than she'd seemed at first, that she cared for him. He'd *allowed* himself to fall for her lies. What a fool!

The sight that had met him as he opened the door was emblazoned on his brain and he couldn't think past it. Antonia in Dexter's arms, her hands on his shoulders. His mouth on her neck. Rafe couldn't believe he'd stopped at hauling the bastard off her. Every impulse had urged him to pound Dexter till he was a bruised and bloodied heap.

He feared what he might do if he succumbed to the impulse for blood. It was only that which had given him the strength to hold back.

Knowing Antonia had been in another man's embrace made him want to vomit. Or rage. Or commit violence.

His fist slammed down again on the sill and pain radiated from the point of impact. Rafe welcomed it. Anything to drag him back to the present, away from the lurid image branded into his brain.

He turned, needing an outlet for the angry energy shooting through him. Something glittered on the carpet. He frowned, identifying it as the trinket he'd given her. The brooch she'd accepted with such apparent pleasure.

He strode straight past it and stopped in front of her. He was itching for an argument. Antonia owed him that much, since he didn't trust himself to confront his father without killing him.

'What have you got to say for yourself?'

She refused to look up, remaining stubbornly silent.

Rafe's chest heaved with barely suppressed fury. He needed an outlet for his wrath. He shoved his fisted hands into his pockets and stared down at her.

Her head was downcast, but he could see she

was pale. Ashen, even. Her features were so still he could barely make out her breathing. Her hands were clasped in her lap, their hold so tight her fingers were white.

Rafe frowned as, unbidden, memory blindsided him. Antonia by her father's grave. So controlled, so cold he'd thought she felt nothing. Only later had he discovered it was a façade she'd adopted to hide the pain deep inside.

A shard of doubt pierced his certainty.

'Look at me,' he ordered.

She didn't move.

'Antonia!'

When she refused to meet his gaze he cupped her chin in his hand. Her flesh was cool to the touch. He lifted her head. Drowning brown eyes met his. They were huge, staring blindly as if she didn't see him.

Foreboding corkscrewed through him at that vacant look. His certainty crumbled a fraction. But he'd been fooled by her before. He wouldn't be gulled a second time. Especially now he knew how potent were her feminine wiles.

'Haven't you got something to say to me?' He was damned if he was going to let her off the hook.

'Is it true?' she whispered, and he had to lean forward to hear her. 'Are you Stuart Dexter's son?'

Rafe straightened, his hand falling away from her.

'What the hell's that got to do with anything?' He wasn't here to recount his life story.

'So it's true.' Her voice was devoid of inflection, and her face could have been that of a beautiful, lifeless mannequin. Her eerie detachment made Rafe's neck prickle. If this was a con job it was remarkably effective.

'Don't you think you owe me an apology?' All that mattered was that he'd found her in his father's arms.

'What for?' There was a spark of energy in her voice this time. 'For not having the strength to fight him off? For not screaming loudly enough?'

Rafe scowled down at her. 'You weren't screaming.' Though even as he spoke he remembered the muffled sound of *something* through the solid door.

Her chin tilted higher in a look he hadn't seen in weeks. The ice queen was back.

'If you can't tell the difference between a lovers' tryst and sexual assault, that's not my problem.'

Sexual assault? She had to be kidding. She must have known what Dexter wanted when she'd come in here with him.

'Or do you think I'd willingly submit to *this*?' She yanked her jacket back to reveal a gaping tear in her dress. There was a livid red mark, already purpling, on her slim shoulder, and one at the base of her neck. Bite marks.

It was like receiving a stupefying blow to the stomach. Rafe's belly cramped as he absorbed the shock.

'No!' She shrank back in her chair, jerking her jacket back over her shoulder as he reached out instinctively towards her, to soothe his fingers over the broken skin.

Rafe froze, reading fear in her eyes. Of him? He'd never touch her in anger. Hadn't he waited to master his emotions before confronting her?

'Don't…touch me,' she whispered. It took only the desperate plea in her husky voice to convince him.

In that instant the last of his rage bled away, leaving Rafe stranded in the knowledge of his own inadequacy. He hadn't protected her. He'd raged at her when he should have held her close and comforted her.

His mind raced back to the moment he'd pulled Dexter away and she'd stood alone, hair mussed and dress dishevelled. There'd been a light in her eyes when she'd seen him. He recognised it now as relief. And desperation in her voice. Yet in his fury he hadn't looked or listened properly. He'd seen Antonia in his father's arms and fury had ousted common sense.

A leaden weight pressed down on his chest, seizing his lungs so his breath laboured. *Guilt.*

He hadn't believed her when she'd needed him.

Rafe hunkered down. She avoided him, looking to one side. Undeterred, he took her hands in his. They were shaking. Antonia was in shock.

'It's all right,' he murmured, pitching his voice low, as he would to a frightened child. 'You're safe now.'

Silence.

'I'm sorry, Antonia. I went crazy when I saw him with you.' He paused. 'I should have believed you immediately.'

She turned and looked at him. But there was no connection there. No softening. Nothing.

'Did you hear me?' There was desperation in his voice. 'I believe you. I know you weren't willing.'

Rusty laughter cracked the air. 'Well, thank you for that, Rafe. You can't imagine how good that makes me feel.'

Rafe frowned as he heard the hint of hysteria. The tremor in her hands was growing worse. He straightened and lifted her in his arms, tucking her in close.

'Come on, Antonia. It's time to go home.'

Home. The word echoed in Antonia's head as she dried herself after the longest, hottest shower in history. She felt as if she'd never be clean again. Though whether from Stuart Dexter's filthy touch or Rafe's razor-sharp accusations, she didn't know.

Silly how she'd begun thinking of the apartment as home, despite her lifelong yearning for a little house. Some place with a garden, neighbours, a sense of community—the things she'd missed out on as she'd traipsed around Europe with her parents.

This could never be home.

Despite the fact that Rafe had turned up the heating, Antonia donned warm trousers, a soft flannel shirt and a thick sweater. The cold had got into her bones.

He was waiting in the sitting room. Even knowing what he thought of her, realising how pathetically far-fetched were her fantasies of love and trust, her heart pattered faster at the sight of his strong profile.

'Antonia. There you are.' He strode over, but halted a few paces away, his expression unreadable. 'I made coffee.' He gestured to the low table in front of a massive suede sofa. A pang of sensation pierced her as she remembered making love with him there one evening, when he'd been so urgent they hadn't made it to the bedroom.

She sat in a nearby chair and poured herself a steaming mug. Mercifully, her hands didn't shake any more.

'Thank you,' she said, and turned to look out at the vista of London spread before them. She'd miss this view, she realised dully.

She sipped the strong coffee. So much nicer than the sickly sweet tea he'd pressed on her earlier.

'We need to talk.' He sounded grim.

'Yes.' She'd spent the trip back to London psyching herself for the discussion they had to have. His brooding silence in the sports car should have made her a nervous wreck, but she'd been so grateful he hadn't wanted to talk then.

'I'm sorry,' he said, sitting on the sofa, leaning forward to catch her eye. 'Truly sorry. I don't know what got into me. I found you together and I just saw red.'

He was genuine. She could see it in his eyes. But it was too late for apologies. What good was sorry when he'd revealed how little he truly thought of her?

'Can you forgive me?'

'It doesn't matter now.' He didn't trust her. He saw her only as a possession he'd bought and which he didn't want to share. *That* was what mattered.

She shrugged and changed the subject. 'It's true. You're his son, aren't you?'

'Yes.' Rafe leaned back in his chair, looking as weary as she felt. 'He's my father.'

'And?' She waited, knowing there was more.

'I'd never seen him until a few months ago,' he said in a cool voice. 'He was the reason I went to the Alps.'

She remembered Rafe's adamantine hardness when they'd met, his sense of urgency. In her naïvety she'd put it down to his determination to get what he wanted: her in his bed. Now she wondered.

'You know what my…father is. A vulture personally, and professionally too.' He shot her a direct look. 'I don't know how he got involved in your mother's charity, but take my advice and have him removed. His practices are dubious, if not downright criminal.'

'Go on.' She sensed Rafe was prevaricating. As if he didn't want to talk about this.

He got to his feet and stalked over to the windows, his hands in his trouser pockets.

'My mother was his PA—young, naïve, but very, very good at her job. He poached her from a colleague and then set about seducing her.' He paused. 'She was in love, swept off her feet. She was waiting for his proposal when she learned he was marrying someone else. Someone with enough money to keep him in the style he wanted.'

Rafe turned and shot her a quick look from under lowered brows. 'That was when she shared the news she'd been waiting to break to him—that she was pregnant.'

Antonia's heart sank. She knew already where this was heading. 'How old was she?'

'Just twenty.' He turned to stare out into the distance, his broad shoulders hunched. 'He told her to get an abortion. Once that *inconvenience* was out of the way they could continue their affair, despite his new bride.'

Antonia shuddered, knowing Dexter was that callous.

'She refused, so he turned her away without a reference. He put it about that she was unstable and had been caught ripping off the petty cash account. He blackened her name so she couldn't work here. Not in the finance sector.'

Rafe paced.

'Mum got as far away as she could. She started afresh in Australia. But she had a difficult pregnancy and no family support. She kept working when she shouldn't have, saving for when the babies arrived.'

'Babies?'

'She was expecting twins.'

Something about the silence at the end of that sentence prevented her from asking more.

'Unfortunately she overdid it, working till she was exhausted. She collapsed on the job, succumbing to a virus. The result was complications and the early onset of labour. Only one child survived.'

He seemed so detached, yet Antonia could detect a wealth of pain in him.

'She blamed herself for my brother's death till the day she died. She felt guilt for something that wouldn't have happened if she'd had proper care and support!'

Antonia heard his grief, and sensed his loss was still raw. She wanted to reach out to him, but she didn't dare.

'We had a decent life. Short on cash, but happy.' He paused. 'Then she was diagnosed with a degenerative illness. It was long, slow and painful.'

Antonia's heart squeezed as she remembered the look on his face when he'd talked of being his mother's carer. Her instinct was to put her arms round him, despite today's events. But he'd never looked more distant.

'I vowed I'd make lots of money and find a cure for her.' His lips twisted in a self-deprecating curl. 'Unfortunately a cure wasn't possible, but at least her last years were comfortable.'

Rafe tasted bitter defeat on his tongue at the thought of how useless his wealth had been. For all his hard work, his determination, his sheer *refusal* to have her give in, she'd slipped away, worn out too early by stress and overwork even before the illness took her.

He stared at the cityscape, not seeing it, remembering instead the information he'd uncovered. Of how Dexter had not only discarded her but been deliberately culpable in exacerbating those years of pain. He'd shortened her life.

'Recently I discovered she'd been in touch with Dexter. Once during her pregnancy, pleading with him to take her back. She loved him, despite what he'd done.'

He paused, still finding that hard to stomach. But then what did he know of romantic love? Just enough never to trust in it! It was a delusion for the unwary.

'He threatened legal action. It was a masterpiece of bluff. If she'd pursued a paternity suit he'd have had to acknowledge me, but it wasn't money she wanted.'

He paused, his fists hardening. 'She wrote later, when she found out how ill she was. She was terrified she'd die while I was young, with no family to take me in. She'd discovered he had no legitimate children and suggested he build a relationship with me against the day she was gone.'

Rafe shook his head in disbelief, knowing she'd swallowed her pride and asked for financial assistance that time, since it had been such a struggle to support her son.

'His answer was curt to the point of insult.' Rafe was still amazed Dexter's lawyers had let him send something so inflammatory. 'He even despatched some goons to make sure she got the message to leave him alone.'

Rafe recalled the late-night visit by dark-suited men with lethally determined voices. He'd been a kid, but he'd stood by his mother, refusing to leave. He'd looked into their grim faces and understood genuine menace for the first time. They hadn't resorted to physical violence. They hadn't needed to. Their intentions had been clear.

That night Rafe and his mother had left their rented home of more than a decade, taking only what they could carry, giving up the friends and the job that had supported them.

'For the next few years we kept on the move, in case Dexter's *associates* looked us up again. Without consistent care or a permanent job my mother's health deteriorated faster than it should. That was Dexter's fault.' Even now the word *father* tasted like poison on his tongue.

He swung around to meet Antonia's compassionate gaze.

'If he'd had a skerrick of common humanity she wouldn't have had to work herself to the bone in dead-end jobs. She'd have had the strength to fight for her life.'

His words tailed away in futile regret. Nothing could bring his mother back. But he could sure as hell make the man who'd betrayed her then hounded her to an early grave pay.

'I came to Europe to get revenge on Stuart Dexter.'

Antonia saw the cruel glitter of pure hatred in his eyes. It was a face that scared her. A remorseless face, belonging to a man driven by the most destructive of emotions. No trace of the warm, caring man she'd thought she'd discovered.

How had she fooled herself that he felt tenderness for her? This man wasn't capable of it. *Nothing* was as important to Rafe Benton as revenge. There was no place in his life for anything as positive as a loving relationship. She'd never *meant* anything to him. Not really. She was merely a convenience.

Her chest tightened as she realised how pathetic she'd been, dreaming of a future together. Their shared joy if, perhaps, her instincts here right and she was pregnant.

She shuddered. Even if there *was* a baby, there'd be no shared joy, no mutual love. No happily-ever-after. How could she expect him to love her child when he was wrapped up in hate and vengeance?

That was no sort of father for any child.

Pain radiated out through her numb body, bringing it to aching life.

'And me?' Her voice was hoarse. 'Where do I fit in?'

Rafe focused on her, as if seeing her for the first time. He sat down opposite her and drew a deep breath.

'I saw you with Dexter—saw how obsessed he was,' Rafe murmured, in that voice which still had the power to unravel her. 'Only two things matter to him. Wealth and satisfying his libido. He goes to extraordinary lengths to pursue any woman he's set on possessing. It's a fixation.'

Rafe waited, as if watching for her reaction. But hurt held Antonia so taut she knew her face was immobile.

'Go on,' she breathed.

'I planned to use that to destroy him: remove his wealth, his business, his reputation. In just a few more weeks Dexter will be insolvent.' Rafe paused, his gaze shifting. 'And I decided to take the woman who currently means more to him than his long-suffering wife ever could. The woman who lets him fantasise that he's young and virile again.' Sky-blue eyes met her. 'I took you.'

Shock exploded inside. It felt as if he'd punched a hole right through her.

Rafe had *never* wanted her for herself! Even the blast of attraction she'd felt when they met had been one-sided. She'd just been a lever to tip the scales in his favour—a tool for revenge.

Her breath caught in her chest and she had to focus on drawing more oxygen into her body as her head spun.

The lovemaking they'd shared, the intimacy she'd believed meant far more than sex, had been just a perk to him. If you paid for a woman—even one chosen because your *father* had the hots for her—why not make the most of her?

In her weaker moments she'd almost been tempted to find his single-mindedness in pursuing her exciting. That a man wanted her so much should be testimony to the strongest of attractions, if only physical.

Yet even *that* had been a sham.

A ball of hot, choking emotion rose in Antonia's throat. Bile burnt the back of her mouth as she grabbed the arms of her chair in a panicked grip. She would *not* break down now. Not in front of him.

Frantically she searched his face for a sign of remorse. She found only rigid determination.

Antonia gagged over the swelling nausea.

'You're like him,' she whispered. She hadn't wanted to believe it. The knowledge was a death knell to all her fragile hopes.

Rafe lifted one dark satanic brow, looking more like Dexter than ever. Searing pain lanced her breast and she knew it was her heart breaking. She'd deluded herself into believing this was a man she could love.

'You're just the same. *Like father, like son.*'

'You've got to be kidding! I'm nothing like that bastard.' Disbelief held Rafe motionless.

He who'd worked his way to success through sheer effort, determination and a well-honed natural talent. He who'd never broken the law in his life, never shirked a responsibility.

'Didn't you hear what I said?' He surged to his feet. 'Don't you understand yet what sort of man Dexter is?'

'Oh, I understand all right. Believe me, the likeness between you two is so blinding I wonder I never saw it before.' Her face was pale as milk, but her eyes flashed topaz fire.

Rafe shook his head. If he responded to that insult he'd say something he'd regret. What had got into her?

'I'm sorry, Antonia. I know this is a shock to you.' That had to be it. She was traumatised from Dexter's attack. Not thinking straight. He'd bruised her ego, revealing how she'd been part of a bigger plan. He shoved his hand through his hair, realising that perhaps he should have trusted her with some of the truth a little earlier.

She laughed—a horrible, jerky sound that jarred every nerve alert. Hysteria? No. She was too calm for that. Too calm all round. A flicker of anxiety flared in his gut.

'Don't apologise,' she said, with all the hauteur of a princess. 'It's a relief finally to hear the truth and know exactly where I stand.'

Rafe frowned, disliking that tone. 'There's more to it than that—'

'I'm sure there is. No doubt your revenge took months of planning. You must have worked hard at it. But I've heard enough.'

She got to her feet so slowly he wondered if Dexter had injured her in their scuffle.

'Are you all right?'

Her brows arched, and for a moment a shadow of emotion flashed across her face. Then it was gone, hidden behind that distant demeanour he'd worked so hard to break down.

'I'm fine,' she lied, tipping her jaw to the defiant angle he knew so well. The way she stood, gripping the back of her chair with hands as tight as talons, the way she swayed slightly, as if unsteady, gave her away.

He took a step towards her.

'No!' The raw emotion in her voice stopped him in his tracks. 'Don't touch me.' It was a plea, not an order.

'Antonia.' He lowered his voice to a soothing murmur. 'Let me take care of you.' She needed him to look after her. And, damn it, he wanted to, despite her defiant air. He couldn't bear to see her like this.

'You've got to be joking.' Her mouth thinned to a flat line of distaste that pulled him up short. 'I'd as soon trust myself to your father's ministrations.'

'Now, hold it right there! You're getting ridiculous!' That anyone, particularly the woman with whom he'd shared so much of himself, could seriously compare him to Stuart Dexter was the ultimate insult.

'Ridiculous, am I?' Antonia jammed her hands on her hips and glared at him.

Despite his annoyance, he couldn't help appreciating the superb picture she made. She was glorious when roused. Rafe felt a tug of desire tighten his belly and thighs.

'You're both utterly selfish. So absorbed in getting what *you* want that you don't give a damn about the consequences for anyone else.'

'That's pure fantasy.' Anger burred his voice and he made an effort to relax. 'Dexter is amoral. His only interest is in pleasing himself.'

She shook her head. 'And you're not? You have this grand plan for vengeance and you do whatever it takes to make it work. *Use* whoever you must. The fact that you're taking advantage of innocent people—'

'Hardly innocent,' he murmured, furious at being challenged on a point of honour. 'Much as I admire you, lover, you *did* agree to my terms, didn't you? It was *your* choice to take up my offer and accept my money.'

The money she'd screwed out of him, he reminded himself bitterly. Though lately that hadn't seemed to matter. Now, though, the thought of it fuelled his anger.

'My *choice*? I never had a choice. You were black-mailing me with those debts.'

Rafe stilled. Yes, he'd bought her debts. Yes, he'd held them over her head, determined to persuade her to agree. But it hadn't been that which had made her comply. It had been the lure of more money that he'd promised. That and the attraction that had blazed like wildfire between them. No matter how she'd tried to deny it, there'd been no mistaking that sensual pull.

'Just like your father. He was going to use black-mail too.' She stared at him, unwavering, and something dropped inside him at the look in her eyes. 'He stole from the Foundation and made it look like my father had done it. That's why I was so desperate for money. To pay back the missing funds.' Her mouth twisted in a spasm that drew Rafe's belly tight. 'My father wasn't around to protect his reputation, so I had to do it for him.'

Aghast, he stood silent, absorbing her words. Dexter had done that? Put her in that position?

'That's why you wanted the money up-front?'

She nodded. 'I needed it straight away so I could transfer it before an audit.'

'Why didn't you tell me?' he blazed. 'If I'd known…' Rafe's words petered out as he realised she couldn't have known he'd have helped her out even though she was a stranger.

'Why would I tell *you*, another man trying to force me into sex?' Anger slurred her words, she spat them out so fast. 'You'd only have used it to your advantage somehow.'

'That's preposterous.' But ice slid down his spine as he realised how untenable her position must have been. How much she'd needed a champion. How he'd taken satisfaction in forcing her to submit to his plan and his wishes.

Silence reigned as he met her glowing eyes and read the truth and the disdain there. It was a new and unsettling experience to feel as if perhaps he deserved it.

'No. What's preposterous is that I didn't see the connection between the two of you before. You're both ruthless and self-absorbed. He steals and lies to get what he wants, and you've spent months totally absorbed in plotting revenge, using whatever means you can to win.'

She paused long enough to heave in an uneven breath.

'You're both blackmailers. Your father views women as sex objects and so do you. Where do you get off, offering a complete stranger money to sleep with you?'

Rafe's skin tightened as she aimed her words like darts. Dull heat spread across his neck.

'How do you think it feels, knowing that the man I've been…intimate with was only motivated by revenge?'

His stomach muscles clenched at the way she said 'intimate', as if it was something dirty.

'He said it today,' she continued remorselessly. *'Like father, like son.* He seemed almost proud of it.' She rubbed her hands over her arms, as if to counter a chill that Rafe couldn't feel. 'He was offering to keep me in style once you'd tired of me. *Keep me in the family.'*

Nausea rocked him, a sucker punch to the gut. When Rafe got his hands on his filthy excuse for a father…

'Where are you going?' It took him a moment to realise she was walking away.

'I'm leaving. I'm not staying to serve out my time. If you've got a problem with that, sue me. I never want to see you again.'

Every instinct told him to go after her, to comfort her, to explain. But his clamouring need for her was overridden by the stark truth written in her face.

She hated him. And with cause. Even the attraction between them, the sexual awareness that had been his excuse for forcing her into intimacy, seemed ephemeral now. It had held him in its thrall and he'd persuaded himself she'd felt it from the first too. But she hadn't…

Rafe spun on his heel and strode out of the apartment. He had no idea where he was going. Nowhere would be far enough to escape the appalling truths she'd revealed.

CHAPTER FOURTEEN

ANTONIA sipped her orange juice in the warm Italian sunshine and let her eyelids droop as she relaxed for the first time, it seemed, in weeks. She'd arrived early for her appointment, and these few moments of peace in the villa's private courtyard were just what she needed.

This last trip had been demanding—a whistlestop tour for an extended-family group. Pity the money bulging in their wallets hadn't made up for their unpleasant personalities.

If she could afford it she'd give up this job and find something else. But she didn't have time. She needed to get some money behind her, quickly. Antonia slid a hand over her still flat stomach and felt tears spring to her eyes as regret welled for all that might have been. For the dream she'd once cherished—her, Rafe and their baby, a loving family.

She'd had no choice. She'd done the right thing in leaving. How could she have stayed with a man who'd given himself over to the poisonous fantasy of revenge? Who'd used her so heartlessly? So cold-bloodedly?

How could a man like Rafe, intelligent, clever, warm and caring behind the tycoon façade, have fallen into that trap? No matter how appalling Stuart Dexter's behaviour, why hadn't Rafe been able to see that pursuing vengeance was turning him into the sort of man he despised?

Then there was the small fact that he didn't love her. Would never love her. Familiar pain twisted inside as it had every day since she'd left him. Every empty day since he'd let her go with not a word of protest. Part of her had expected him to follow, to sweep her into his arms and refuse to let her leave. But he hadn't cared enough.

She sobbed herself to sleep every night, crying for what she'd never have. The wall of protective ice round her heart had finally broken and she felt raw from grief.

Yet now she had a reason to be strong. She needed to pull herself together and concentrate on the future.

Rafe stood in the shadows of the courtyard, watching her. She was even more beautiful than he remembered, her profile perfection, her body sheer invitation, even covered in the sedate suit she wore for work.

How would she react when she found her new client was the man she'd spurned a month ago?

His stomach churned; his pulse hammered. The sensation had become familiar these past weeks, as he'd come to terms with what she'd said and realised how small were his chances of persuading her to come back. He was a desperate man.

Abruptly he stepped out of the shadows and into the sunlight. He couldn't take this waiting any longer.

'Antonia.'

'Rafe?' The shock of hearing his voice jerked her out of her reverie. It was *him*, standing right in front of her. Eyes bluer than the sky stared down at her from that face she knew so well.

Her heart accelerated into an uneven tattoo at the stunning picture he made, gilded by sunlight. He was all masculine angles and hard planes, tall and powerful and utterly magnetic. She barely stifled the need to reach out to him.

How pathetic was she?

'I missed you.' His voice, deep and warm, rumbled across her skin, and a flitter of joy shivered through her.

I missed you too. But she couldn't say it.

'I'd have thought you'd have another woman to warm your bed by now.' Anguish ripped through her at the idea, but she needed to remind herself to stay firm.

He shook his head, eyes never leaving hers. 'I'm

not interested in any other woman. You must know that.'

Antonia was silent. He'd let her walk out of his life without a word of protest. If he'd cared he'd have tried to persuade her to stay. She knew the truth. He'd never really wanted *her*. That knowledge was a cold, suffocating weight on her chest, making it hard to draw breath.

'I've done my time as your mistress. I'm not going back to that.'

'I didn't for a moment think you would.'

Antonia's heart nosedived. He'd confirmed it, as she'd known he would—he didn't want her back.

Why did it hurt so much, hearing it from his lips? She bit down on a suddenly trembling lip.

'Why are you here?' Every moment he stood there it grew harder to maintain this shell of composure. She feared she couldn't keep up the pretence. Not when her heart was breaking at seeing him so close, so unattainable. She knew she shouldn't want him, but was unable to suppress the craving.

He dragged out a chair and sat in front of her. His knees almost brushed hers. His powerful hands flexed on his thighs. The scent of his skin reached her, making her nostrils flare and her nipples tighten.

No! It was too much. She made to stand.

'Wait.' His hand hovered close to hers.

'I'm here to meet a client.' Antonia looked at her

watch. Surely she had the time right? The message had said ten. The housekeeper expected her.

'I know.' That was all he said, but suddenly she knew. It was *Rafe* who had requested her for this job. Rafe who'd booked a personalised tour through Italy.

'Marcus Paulson—'

'Is my agent.' He paused. 'I knew if I made the arrangements myself you wouldn't agree to meet me.'

He was dead right. Even now, knowing what he was, how he'd used her, she found herself wanting to stay.

'I have to go. I can't—'

'I need to talk to you, Antonia.' His eyes clouded, as if this was as painful for him as for her. 'To explain.'

Automatically she shook her head.

'Please.'

The single word stilled her movements and she subsided in her chair. There was such sincerity in his expression, a rough edge of discomfort in his voice. The problem was that even now she could barely resist him.

'Thank you.'

For a moment she thought he was going to reach out, and her heartbeat revved. She told herself it wasn't disappointment she felt when he didn't.

'I'm sorry,' he said at last. 'Sorry for everything. You were right. I behaved terribly. As bad as my...

father. Worse, I prided myself that I was dealing out justice for his sins, yet I didn't see the damage I inflicted. On you.'

He thrust his hand through his immaculate dark hair in a gesture that made him look oddly vulnerable. Silently Antonia cursed herself for responding to it, for wanting to reach out to him.

'I forced you into an impossible situation and there was no excuse. I let my bitterness cloud my judgement. I convinced myself you were the sort of mercenary party girl I despised. The sort of woman I've been fending off for years. I should have guessed the truth. You were too honest, too decent for that.' He drew in a long, slow breath. 'I treated you abominably.'

'I…' What could she say? That in her heart she'd already forgiven him? She blinked back tears, unable to prevent the wish that she'd met him *now*, not when he'd been obsessed with vengeance.

'Don't cry, Antonia.' He took her hand and chafed it. His touch felt so good she didn't have the strength to tug out of his hold.

'I'm not crying.' She reserved that for the lonely solitude of her single bed.

Silently he reached out and stroked her cheek. She felt dampness there and was horrified. She'd been so determined that he'd never see her weak.

'Of course you're not.' He pulled out a large white handkerchief and wiped her cheek as she blinked back the welling tide. 'You've been so brave, Antonia, so strong.'

She almost convinced herself she read approval in his cerulean gaze. A glow of warmth sparked inside her.

'I need to tell you about Stuart Dexter.'

Her shoulders slumped. He'd come to talk about Dexter?

'It took me a long time to deal with the truth,' Rafe said. 'I'd been fixated on revenge—though I called it justice—for so long it was hard to shift my perspective.' His mouth twisted in a grim line. 'You did that for me. When you told me I was like him I couldn't believe it. I didn't want to believe it.'

His hold tightened but she didn't complain. She'd longed to take back the accusation almost as soon as she'd made it. Even then she'd known it wasn't true. Rafe had an inner core of decency Dexter had never possessed.

'It was only when I discovered you were right about the man I'd become that I realised I had to drop it.'

'You've given up your pursuit of him?' It seemed unbelievable. Rafe had been so single-minded.

He shrugged. 'Not completely. After what he did to you I couldn't let him walk away scot-free, so I compromised.'

Antonia's brows puckered. 'I don't understand.'

Rafe smiled, and she saw a trace of the ruthless tycoon in that satisfied expression.

'I stopped trying to play God. Dexter's in so much difficulty he'll go under soon without me interfering. But I made sure the information my team had dug up on his dubious business practices was available to the authorities. They were eager to see the documentary evidence.' Rafe leaned towards her, his expression serious. 'Let them bring him to justice. There are more important things in life. I wash my hands of him.' He paused. 'Unless you want to press charges for assault? If you do, I'll back you all the way.'

She shook her head. The last thing she wanted was to revisit the past.

'I knew the damage he'd done my mother, and how he'd tried to manipulate and then force you. It made me wonder what life had been like for the woman he married.'

Antonia blinked. 'It did?'

His mouth thinned to a sombre line. 'I realised how lucky my mother had been despite everything. Being married to my father would have been infinitely worse.'

His gaze grew unfocused, as if he saw things she couldn't, and Antonia realised how devastating it must be for a man of Rafe's pride to acknowledge a louse like Dexter as his father.

She wrapped her fingers around his in a tiny gesture of comfort. Instantly his eyes zeroed in on hers in a look that made her feel hot. She tried to slip her hand away, but his hold tightened. Was that a satisfied curve at one corner of his mouth, or just her imagination?

'What did you do?' she asked, suddenly breathless.

He lifted his shoulders in an offhand movement. 'There wasn't much I could do. I made sure the house was in his wife's name, so she'll have somewhere to live when he loses everything else. And I secured an annuity for her.'

'You did that? You don't even know the woman.'

'We've met,' he said. 'And it was the least I could do. Call it a family duty to pick up the pieces in his wake. Besides, it felt…right.'

'Oh, Rafe.' Emotion welled. He really *had* changed.

'What?' His brows arrowed down as he watched her.

'I'm glad.' Even though it made the pain of knowing he'd never want her even more poignant.

'Really?'

His look was so intense it stripped away the last of her defences. She couldn't afford to let him guess how she felt about him. All she had left was her pride.

'Yes. I'm pleased for you. You can move on.' She hitched her chin higher. 'And so can I.'

For what seemed a full minute he stared into her eyes, as if probing everything she tried to hide.

'In that case we can talk about this tour.'

She jerked back in her seat.

'You're not serious!' He couldn't expect her to escort him around Italy on a month's personalised tour. That would be too cruel.

She'd have to deal with him in the future. The secret she carried made that inevitable. But not now. Not yet. The pain was still too raw. She wasn't ready.

'I've never been more serious about anything,' he murmured, capturing her other hand and holding it in his.

Antonia felt the blood pulse fast through her hands, through his, their heartbeats in time.

'Spend the next month with me?'

She shook her head so vigorously she felt her hair slide loose of its pins. 'I can't.'

'Why not? Wouldn't you enjoy a holiday together, getting to know each other properly?'

'No!' Antonia was aghast. She wanted it too much. Already knew him too well. That was the problem. She couldn't bear to be with Rafe, knowing her feelings weren't reciprocated.

'Not even if I told you I loved you?'

Her eyes rounded in astonishment and her heart faltered. She didn't have time to absorb his words for suddenly he moved, pulling her up into the circle of his arms. She tried to back away, but his embrace was like warm steel, keeping her close.

'I don't believe you.'

'I love you, Antonia. Believe it. Have I ever lied to you?'

'But when…?'

'Ages ago. I didn't know it was love. I thought it was plain old-fashioned lust. It wasn't till you walked out on me that I realised I'd lost the one thing that made my life whole.'

The hunger, the pain in his eyes almost convinced her.

'But you didn't come after me.'

'Would you have taken me?' He shook his head. 'You needed space. And I needed to make some changes before I came after you. You painted a frightening picture of what I'd become. How could I ask you to take on a man like that? I needed time to sort myself out.'

Antonia felt a ripple of excitement deep inside. Could it be true? She tried to think sensibly about what he said but cogent thought was almost impossible. Then she looked into his dear, stern, worried face and realised he was absolutely serious.

Rafe loved her!

'Say you'll come, Antonia. Give me a month to show you how much I love you. A month to convince you that you care for me too. *I know you do.*' His gaze was mesmerising.

'I do,' she whispered. 'I love you, Rafe. I—'

'Antonia…' His lips closed on hers, and any thought of speech fled. All the dialogue they needed was here, in their entwined bodies. He held her so close, yet so tenderly, his hands sliding possessively over her as if he'd never get enough of her. There was magic in their kiss, in the hot, slow dance of their tongues, in the luscious sharing of intimacy. Antonia gave herself up to the ecstasy of being in the arms of the man she loved. And who loved her.

'I don't deserve you,' he whispered against her lips, when they finally broke apart to gasp down some air.

'Don't be absurd.'

'It's true.' Blue eyes bright with passion met hers. 'But I'm not saint enough to deny myself. I wanted you from the moment I saw you, and I'll *never* let you go.'

'Rafe. You don't have to say that. I know it was just because Dexter wanted—'

His finger on her lips stopped her. 'Let's not mention him again. But as for wanting you, my darling, you should know that revenge was just the excuse I needed to make a move on you. Even if he hadn't been there I'd have pursued you. I saw you and I wanted you. I had to have you. And nothing's changed except that now I understand how much you mean to me.'

When Rafe looked at her like that Antonia found it hard to breathe. Burgeoning joy robbed her of words. He'd wanted her from the first? Just as she had wanted him?

'Say you'll marry me,' he demanded. 'We'll make this our honeymoon. When it's over we'll look for a house together—anywhere you want.'

She shook her head, still stunned at the sight of her

determined lover so needy, so…desperate. Emotion swirled deep inside as she met his eyes.

'Antonia. You can't refuse!' His voice was raw with shock. His hands tightened possessively.

'No, I'm not refusing.' Her voice was uneven, whether with tears or welling laughter she didn't know. 'I'd love to marry you, Rafe.'

He pulled her close, his eyes glittering as he bent to kiss her. But she held him off, reaching out to take his hand and slip it between them to rest low on her belly.

'The sooner we get ready for this little one's arrival, the better.'

'A baby?' He was still for heartbeat, then he scooped her up in his arms and twirled her round, his deep laugh echoing across the wide courtyard. Antonia had never heard a more joyous sound.

'Have I told you how wonderful you are, Antonia?'

She grinned, the last of her doubts dissolving like shadows at midday. 'I didn't do it by myself, you know.'

He stopped, his eyes meeting hers unerringly. 'I love you, Antonia Malleson.'

'And I love you, Rafe Benton.'

There in the citrus-scented sun, the words sounded like vows. The echo of distant church bells rose in the air. For a long moment they stared into each other's eyes, feeling love surround them. Then Rafe turned with her in his arms and strode towards the open doors.

'Where are we going?'

The devil was in his eyes as he smiled down at her. 'To anticipate our honeymoon.'

* * * * *